MY LIFE IN THE SILVER SCREEN

by the same author

HOW TO LIVE UNDER LABOUR
THE LEFT
TO BUILD THE PROMISED LAND
HOW TO BE A MINISTER
RENEWAL: LABOUR'S BRITAIN IN THE 1980S

MY LIFE IN
THE SILVER SCREEN

GERALD KAUFMAN

faber and faber
LONDON · BOSTON

First published in 1985
by Faber and Faber Limited
3 Queen Square London WC1N 3AU

Filmset by Goodfellow & Egan, Cambridge
Printed in Great Britain by
Thetford Press
Thetford Norfolk

© Gerald Kaufman, 1985

British Library Cataloguing in Publication Data

Kaufman, Gerald
My life in the silver screen
1. Kaufman, Gerald   2. Statesmen—Great
Britain—Biography
I. Title
941.085′092′4   DA591.K3
ISBN 0-571-13493-9

TO MY PARENTS

In deep gratitude for their irresponsibility in taking me
to the pictures at an age so early that cinema-going
became for me an incurable addiction

CONTENTS

CREDITS

My thanks to: John Gillet and the staff of the British Film Institute library, for confirming (or occasionally confuting) my movie memories; Nonie Cullum, for transforming my almost unreadable first draft into an elegant typescript.

G.K.

I

OPENING TITLES

———

This is where I came in.

Curiously, what I remember most vividly is the smell. It was at its most pervasive in the entrance foyer of the luxurious Ritz picture palace in Vicar Lane, in the centre of Leeds; but it was present in every cinema. I thought at the time that it came from the chocolates on sale, but it was not a chocolate smell. It was pungent, it was heady, it was almost intoxicating. To this day I have no idea what it was or where it came from. It was there then; it is nowhere today. To me, as a child, whatever it was, it was the smell of going to the pictures, the advance signal of the magic ahead.

My first exposure to that magic took place when I was 3 years old. Today every baby is brought up with moving pictures all around it. Half a century ago, there was no visual home entertainment at all. In our home at 31 Roundhay Road, behind the cloth shop that my mother kept to augment the wages earned by my tailor father at Montague Burton's clothing factory at Hudson Road Mills, we had a huge radio, 'the wireless', proudly described by its full title as an Ultra Panther; to this I paid little attention.

There was in addition a highly unreliable gramophone, which had to be cranked by hand and was operated with the aid of cruel-looking needles kept in a tin box. This contrivance was for me a source of misery and fear, since it was employed to play either sad records of sobbing Jewish cantors or a comic item called 'The Laughing Policeman', whose roars of manic hilarity always evoked countervailing wails of terror from me. My much-put-upon brother David, five years older than I and understandably anxious to go and play football with his friends rather than unwillingly fulfil conscript duties as custodian to me, would sometimes play 'The Laughing Policeman' as a form of revenge.

I much preferred books since – precocious to the point of absurdity – by the time I was three I could read quite well, even though I did not understand everything I read. For example, I

13

carefully pronounced the letter 'w' in 'sword', a word of whose meaning I was not really sure.

One day I was told I was being taken to the pictures, and I was left in no doubt that this was an important development in my life. I had heard my parents and my sisters discussing films. I was, however, not sure what these were, just as I was not sure what a sword was and just as I was not sure what clouds were; for a long time I believed that these last were the wires stretching between the high poles stationed along Roundhay Road (not to be confused with the shorter poles which were gas lamps, and which could be caused to light up by the application of a judicious kick).

As my film-going career proceeded through childhood, my older sisters each in turn accepted the responsibility of accompanying me. These were, in descending order of age: Dora who, seventeen years older than I, worked with my father at Burton's factory and who one Friday afternoon brought me home the very first issue of the *Dandy*, with as a free gift a metal facsimile of Korky the Cat; Martha, who went from Lawnswood High School to Leeds Teacher Training College, and who later tried in vain to interest me in the theatre by taking me to see *Peter Pan* at the Grand Theatre; Anne, another teacher-to-be, whose earliest duties were to instruct me in feeding the ducks on Roundhay Park lake; Gertie, then still at school, who sang sweetly to me when I was a baby and then secretly taught me to swear; and – the youngest sister, though still older than David – Hilda, who never at any time forgot to send a birthday card to me or indeed to anybody else. However, on that first and most memorable occasion it was my mother who got me ready, neat and tidy, for my inaugural exposure to the movies.

We walked out of the front door of the shop and crossed the road, but did not wait at the tram stop opposite to where we lived. Instead, we walked down Roundhay Road to the Sheepscar fare stage, thus saving ½d of the fare on the No. 3 tram that took us to 'town' as the central part of Leeds was universally known. We got off at Briggate barrier, a kind of complicated cattle pen in the middle of the road where passengers waited for the noisy, rattling vehicles which, letting off sparks and with a clanging of bells, set off from this main thoroughfare of Leeds for destinations all over the city. Opposite the barrier, a little way down from Matthias Robinson's classy department store on the other side of Briggate, was situated the august Rialto cinema, which I was doomed not to visit very often, since it was demolished far too soon to make way for a branch of Marks & Spencer. The film that initiated me into a delirious lifetime of cinema-going was a Disney cartoon called *The Three Little Pigs*. To this day I can see those plump, self-important creatures up on that huge screen bustling about and singing their feckless ditty, 'Who's afraid of the big bad wolf?' I looked up at the singing and dancing animals, an inexplicable phenomenon far beyond anything I had ever experienced before. I had no idea how they worked, but I was enchanted; I was hooked. I wanted more.

In the years following that initiation, the thousands of pictures I viewed were often of far less pristine innocence. The ritual, however, was invariably the same. An usherette stepped forward. There was always an usherette, whether the cinema was a mean one, its foyer no more than the narrow gap between the entrance from the street and the door leading into the auditorium, or a true picture palace, possibly with an illuminated fountain playing in a space decorated sedately in Art Nouveau style or wildly with jungle plants or a reproduction of certain key features of Mad King Ludwig's demented castle in Neuschwanstein, Bavaria.

Then I entered the darkness. It was a deep darkness, so deep that the usherette's torch was indispensable to progress and, indeed, to the avoidance of possibly serious injury. Even while I was stumbling towards my seat, obediently and entrancedly following the confident beam of the torch, I was already looking up, hypnotized by the immense faces that loomed above all of us – for many were present – from the huge but modestly rectangular screen. The faces were always there because I always entered in the middle of the movie. Attendance was at night-time because there was a popular conviction that going to the pictures during daylight was a sure guarantee of a headache, and only the most egregious risked that. Nowadays it is almost impossible to enter a cinema part-way through the main film. Programmes are separate, seats often allocated individually according to number and row; when the picture ends the exiguous audience is bustled out by the (in the West End of London, at any rate) exotically beautiful Filippino girls who are presumably employed for some utilitarian function but who until that moment have not manifested their presence in any way.

Then it was different. To be sure, the newspaper advertisements

published times when the films were due to begin. These, however, were only studied as a safeguard against the one disaster to
be avoided at all costs: entering the cinema after the big picture
had started its last showing, so losing any chance whatever of
catching up. Otherwise, I went to the pictures not when the
cinema management was ready but when I was, however little
chance there was that my timing would coincide with the start or
finish of any part of the programme.

This universal practice led the most skimpily educated people
to attempt, without considering its nature, an intellectual effort of
the utmost magnitude. The film, probably lasting some ninety
minutes, was well under way, possibly forty minutes of its
running time having already elapsed when I joined it, like a
passenger getting on to a tram long after it had left the terminus.
The characters had been established. Key information about the
plot had already been dispensed. It was now up to me, sitting
there in a daze, to make sense of what I was seeing. The story
would go forward. If it was a murder, the solution and the
identity of the guilty person would be revealed possibly before the
name of the victim was known to the spectator. If it was a love
story, the romantic couple would be united or – very much more
rarely – parted by mournful circumstances, even before they had
met.

The lights would then go up and, blinking, I would try to sort
out what I had seen. I had little time in which to do so. For the
lights would speedily dim again. If I was in a large cinema, an
organist, grinning dementedly and waving with one hand, would
rise from some vault beneath the screen and commence to bore
me to distraction with tunes of the past while, on the screen,
coloured patterns fluctuated and changed. Then would come
what was known in the trade as the second feature or the B movie,
but to me it was simply the other picture, the one I had very likely
not come to see, with actors with names like Barton MacLane or
Penny Singleton. These programme-fillers seemed more often
than not to be set in a logging camp but were sometimes part of a
series, such as 'Blondie' or maybe 'The Bowery Boys', which I
quite enjoyed.

The B movie generally lasted for somewhat over an hour.
When it ended, the lights went up again, frequent intervals being
highly necessary to allow customers to attend to calls of nature
during a programme which in total might last for more than four

hours. There then followed, in no particular order: the trailers, offering morsels of both films being shown next week together with those due the week after; a cartoon, possibly of Mickey Mouse or the much more popular Donald Duck, but quite likely of some other clothed animal; a short feature, not a documentary, for audiences would not tolerate them until the War made them obligatory, but an attenuated little fictional film featuring performers not even as well known as Barton MacLane. There were no advertisements. The fearsome and baneful invasion of the cinema screen by Pearl and Dean and their competitors was yet to come. The lights went on again and, smiling in their spotlight, the ice-cream girls moved among the audiences purveying their wares.

Then, at very long last, the lights dimmed again. The huge curtains swished open, revealing another curtain, this time satiny and frilled, which always startled by rising instead of parting. The screen, illuminated in colour, was revealed. The censor's certificate appeared. Then the lion roared or the searchlights flashed, or the WB shield challenged, or the mountain encircled by stars loomed, or what appeared to be the Statue of Liberty shone her signal, or the World revolved or staccato radio signals sent their message, and the credit titles told me that I was at last to see the first part of what I had come to see.

Right from the beginning I recognized characters starting upon adventures whose outcome I already knew. I nodded with comprehension as some plot element which had puzzled me in its denouement was made clear by its exposition. This act of deduction was not easy, for every few moments my concentration on the screen was interrupted first by the distracting beam of the usherette's torch and then by newcomers stumbling over my feet and impeding my view as they took their places, to be perplexed in their turn by what they saw. Then there arrived the moment at which I had come in. At that point, different of course for each group in the audience, those who had now seen the whole film, though not in the right order, rose to leave. It never occurred to most people to stay a moment longer. They had seen all that was on offer. Now it was time to go.

A very tiny minority, if they had enjoyed the big picture a great deal, might sit on to the end; they were regarded as peculiar. Some might stay and sit the whole programme round again, there being nothing whatever to stop them except their own sense of propriety. Generally this disorderly element consisted of boys. More and more, once I was old enough to decide for myself rather than being under the control of an older relative, it included me. For my days soon became dominated by thoughts of going to the pictures and, once in the cinema, I had literally to be dragged out.

Yet cinema-going was far from being an anti-social activity. Everybody went, and no one more so than the many members of my large family. My sisters were particularly assiduous attenders, and the house resounded with discussion of what they had seen. We even had a goldfish named Nolie after the sad heroine played by Irene Dunne in the weepie musical *Showboat*. At least we confined this manifestation of film fanaticism to a dumb creature. Others named human members of their households after cinema favourites, as is evidenced to this day by the profusion of Garys and Marlenes (followed by Ingrids and Marilyns) which can be found on any electoral register.

It was, however, my parents who not only took me first but took me most. Neither of them could read English, they being pre-First World War immigrants from Poland whose never-ending toil to feed, clothe and house seven children prevented them from finding time to attend a night school and learn methodically the language of the country they had made their home. They spoke the language well enough, but their knowledge of it was aural rather than visual, and they often got words wrong. I had a long battle with my mother before she gave up 'disgusted' in place of 'disgusting' and she never abandoned 'without of friends' as a reference to someone with whom she was not on good terms. My father, as a devout Jew, wanted everyone he admired to be Jewish too and, since this was not possible in a predominantly Gentile society, he would recruit his favourites as honorary Jews, the most prominent being the radio star whom he knew as Wolfie Pickles.

Both of them had a taste for the Yiddish films occasionally shown at our neighbourhood cimema, the Forum in Chapeltown Road, right in the heart of the working-class Jewish population. Chapeltown was just down the road from more affluent Chapel Allerton and far away on the wrong side of the tracks from snobby Moortown and even snootier Alwoodley (to which, when the most moneyed Jews began moving to big detached houses there, their co-religionists of Chapeltown scornfully gave the name Alyidley). Up Grange Avenue I would walk with them, crossing Chapeltown

Road and then turning left for three blocks before arriving at the location which is now occupied by a garage. We would then watch together such masterworks as *The French Lesson*, in which a teacher knowing no French hilariously taught Yiddish to pupils who thought they were being taught French, and *Yiddl Miten Fiddl*, filmed on location in Poland. This sentimental musical's theme tune remained in my head for more than forty years until, weeping, I heard it again in the compilation of Yiddish films called *Almonds and Raisins* which was issued in 1984.

My father's taste in English-speaking films was highly sentimental too. He liked most pictures which featured girls, since he had the generous conviction that all girls were beautiful, which opinion consequently made all girls (and most other people) like him. He was addicted to sensational stories featuring women, of which by far his favourite was Alfred Hitchcock's remake of *The Man Who Knew Too Much*, and to strictly moral stories featuring women, Maureen O'Hara in John Ford's *The Quiet Man* being Doris Day's only rival with a fighting chance. As he grew older he came to admire sloppy stories featuring older men, the prime example being the ineffable Barry Fitzgerald in *Going My Way*, that sanctimonious horror sanctifying a singing priest. My father had no taste whatever, but this failed to trouble him since he did not know you were supposed to have taste or, indeed, that taste was a thing you could have.

My mother went to everything. Of course, she had her favourites too. One was Fritz Lang's *Metropolis*, which she regularly praised, not realizing that it was a cinematic classic (or that there were such things as cinematic classics) but simply including it among the small group of films (others being *The Chocolate Soldier* and items starring Theda Bara) that she had particularly enjoyed. However, the movie she doted on most was a musical which she called 'Fireflight' whose credit title listed it as *The Firefly* and which included the song she liked best in the whole world, the 'Donkey Serenade'. She loved this film even though it starred Jeanette MacDonald, who was known throughout our family as 'the Horse', and she committed the almost unheard-of eccentricity of seeing it no fewer than three times. On one occasion I accompanied my mother to *The Firefly*. I could, however, make nothing of the incomprehensible goings-on on the screen, which featured gypsies and armies and people constantly bursting into song for no explicable reason, and I could not understand why

Jeanette MacDonald was being partnered by a grinning person called Allan Jones instead of her usual companion, the much more respectable Nelson Eddy.

At least once a week my mother would put on her coat, tuck her handbag under her arm and leave the house, generally to go to the Forum, but sometimes to the more distant Clock cinema – she never went to the Gaiety, which was nearer than the Clock, because it was not respectable. Often she would take me with her, and there we would sit, she gazing intently at the screen, her chin slightly raised, her somewhat beaked nose (she had broken it when much younger, her considerable beauty thereby being a little impaired) silhouetted in the beam from the projector into which swirled smoke from the nicotine-addicted audience.

Sometimes the film was chosen by me, possibly a comedy featuring George Formby. More often, it was pot luck. I would sit, cowering in terror at some Gothic romance, such as the film that my mother called 'Vuddery Heights'. Of course, there were avowed horror films, with vampires and zombies, and these terrified me so much that I would hide my eyes. On one occasion, watching what I now know to have been a classic of its time, *The Old Dark House*, I was so filled with dread that I performed an action which was almost unheard of among picture-goers in Chapeltown and which I have only ever repeated three times since (during Cecil B. de Mille's *Samson and Delilah*, a British musical of unparalleled feebleness called *Stars in Your Eyes* and a hard-core pornographic film of unrecorded title): I left the auditorium in the middle of the film.

Emerging, quivering, into the Forum's foyer, I paused for a moment by the illuminated fountain which was still twinkling away there and found, sitting on one of its surrounding seats, none other than my brother David. He had been able to obtain entry this far because, the last showing of the main film being well under way, the guardian whose duty was to scrutinize tickets and tear them in half had gone home. At the sight of me, David – far hardier than I – took in the situation at a glance and, rising from his seat without a word, slipped into the auditorium (its entrance in its turn no longer under the supervision of a torch-bearing usherette) and, quite fairly if with dubious legality, took my place to watch the remainder of the film. It never occurred to me, then or afterwards, to ask what he was doing there in the first place.

My sisters would, if in a good mood, occasionally take me to the movies. This might be to a special treat, such as Shirley Temple in *Bright Eyes*. At the time I thought that I liked Shirley Temple very much indeed, and that I was appalled by her harassment by the bad girl, Jane Withers, who was inserted into this movie in order to provide *Schadenfreude*. Now I know that little Miss Temple really made me sick, and that the lively evil of Miss Withers, who never had a chance of becoming Ambassador to anywhere, was what really made such glutinous films tolerable.

My sisters did not operate on the basis of being indulgent to me. They wanted to enjoy themselves too, and sometimes had an elevated idea of what enjoyment implied. Once, as we were sitting by the coal fire at 31 Roundhay Road, a lively and eventually acrimonious discussion developed between my sister Anne, who had offered to take me to the pictures, and myself. Each of us in turn studied the cinema advertisements in the *Yorkshire Evening Post*. There were at the time fifty-five cinemas functioning in Leeds, but in the view of all members of my family but myself (and at the age of five I was very much too young to have any say in the matter) only local cinemas and those in town (the centre of the city) were within our catchment area. Choice was restricted further by the inability of my sister, on this occasion at any rate, to afford tickets at the cinemas in town. Eventually, I decided quite firmly that I would like to see *One in a Million*, the initial screen exploit of Sonja Henie, the Norwegian performer (to call her an actress would be pressing too hard the boundaries of that word's definition), who looked like a wooden doll but skated like a demented elf. Anne scorned this selection, offering in its stead Chaplin's latest product, *Modern Times*. Even at that early age I regarded Chaplin as the embodiment of smirking tedium, and I declined. My sister, also, refused to change her mind, but had the grace not to go on her own on an outing which after all had been proposed as a treat for me. We therefore stayed ill-temperedly at home. I never did get anyone to take me to see *One in a Million*, just as I could never persuade adults to take me to Leeds Empire to see the Great Lyle (and his Mysteries) accomplishing acts of magic. I did, much later, see *Modern Times*, but by that time my movie experience was considerably greater and I was able to perceive that this Chaplin extravaganza was simply a plagiarism of René Clair's *A Nous la Liberté* which, truth to tell, I did not think much of either.

I could never go to the pictures as often as I liked, since to go as often as I liked would have meant attending at least once a day. Furthermore, my father's devout Jewish orthodoxy meant that I was forbidden to attend children's Saturday matinées. It was only much later, when my mother and I went on holiday to Blackpool without him, that both of us, feeling unbelievably sinful, one Sabbath afternoon sneaked into the Tivoli cinema to see Alice Faye and John Payne in *Hello, Frisco, Hello*, and were never afterwards able to explain why 'You'll Never Know' had become one of our favourite songs.

Accordingly, my interest in the movies was much greater than my attendance. From study of the newspapers I was soon familiar with the structure of film distribution in the city of Leeds. At the junction between the Headrow and Briggate was situated the grandest cinema of all, the Paramount, where you could not only see a programme that took up most of the day but, if you had the money, might also eat a substantial high tea. Its name was surrounded by magical moving lights, a feature which greatly increased both its glamorous attraction and also, somehow, its unattainability. The Paramount naturally showed films made by Paramount Pictures, but eventually was bought by the Odeon chain.

Next in order of importance was the Ritz, owned by the ABC group and the showplace for films made by Warner Brothers and Metro-Goldwyn-Mayer. Warner Brothers for me meant not James Cagney and Edward G. Robinson (the latter was a particular favourite of my father's because he was Jewish without any doubt whatever) in gangster films but Errol Flynn and Olivia de Havilland in *The Adventures of Robin Hood*. I had lost my heart to Miss de Havilland's Maid Marian, but was perplexed as to how she could be the sister of Joan Fontaine, their names being different, unlike those of Priscilla, Rosemary and Lola Lane, who were clearly related. MGM for my mother implied Jeanette Macdonald and Nelson Eddy but, for me, Judy Garland and Mickey Rooney.

I regarded as twins the other cinemas which were what I later learned to call first-run houses. The Majestic in City Square and the Scala in Albion Place were the most important properties owned by what became the Rank Organisation. For reasons I neither then nor subsequently could ever understand, they almost always showed the same programme, details being available in a little printed booklet that I used to collect and study with deep care as soon as I was permitted to walk (I did not have the money for the tram fare) into town.

It was only on the rarest possible occasions that I managed to achieve entry into any of these four auditoria. I did, however, have better luck with the Gaumont and the Assembly Rooms, which were under the same ownership as the Majestic and the Scala, and to which the programmes exhibited at these two more august showplaces would be transferred after a decent interval of two or three weeks. There tickets were considerably cheaper. The Gaumont under earlier proprietors had previously been called the Coliseum, and was still popularly known as the Colly. Even though it too was in town, it was in a fairly shady area and regarded as only marginally respectable. The Assembly Rooms, higher up Briggate than the Paramount-Odeon, was, perhaps because of its aristocratic name – which would have been reminiscent of Bath, if any members of my family had ever heard of Bath or had known what it signified – much more acceptable. This attitude was odd, since the Assembly Rooms was a decidedly shabby place, whose seediness reached its apotheosis many years later when it was sold to new owners, who jazzily renamed it the Plaza and attracted a somewhat specialized clientele by showing semi-pornographic films most of which included the word 'Naked' in the title. It was at the Assembly Rooms that, under the negligent custodianship of my father, I was sick down the collar of a man sitting in front of me, an event which aroused curiously little commotion even from my victim and which may be recorded as the earliest and most decisive example of my film criticism.

Still farther along Briggate was the Tower, to which used to be transmitted the Ritz programmes a few weeks after that superior cinema had finished with them. The Tower was notable for being the only movie-house in town which, in its rear rows, provided double seats in which affectionate couples could sit without the obstacle of an armrest between them. The Tower was cheap enough for me to afford to patronize. When, now nine years old, I was permitted to go to cinemas in town on my own, like many boys of this age I had the difficulty when by myself of being able only to gain admittance to cinemas to see U films. Children had to be accompanied by an adult even if one of the most trivial items on show had an A. Therefore, if there was an A element in the programme, I used to hang around the entrance waiting for a benevolent adult to 'take me in'. All involved in this ritual, including the sniffy lady in the box office, knew the drill. Being taken in involved accosting an adult who was approaching the cinema entrance with a positive air of buying a ticket, and whiningly asking to be allowed to accompany him or her. If consent was obtained, I would hand over my admission money (half-price of course) to the person concerned, who would then buy me my half-price ticket and who would hand it over to me once the ticket-tearing official had dealt with it. We would then part for ever.

It was at the Tower that, hanging about to be 'taken in', I not only obtained the consent of an adult male cinemagoer but even had my ticket bought for me out of his own money by this philanthropist who, in customary fashion, then dispensed with my company the moment we entered the auditorium. This event, unique and unforgettable, was to me such a triumph that I could not get home soon enough to tell my parents about it. To my surprise they did not share my elation, but questioned me closely about this man, unwilling to believe that we had parted company as soon as my ticket had been bought. It was not for some years that I understood why they did not regard this as a totally delightful occurrence, and why they mysteriously but emphatically warned me never to accept such generosity again.

Also in town were two small cinemas which formed a little chain of their own. One was the Tatler on Boar Lane, which showed films whose characters spoke in foreign languages and which was never visited by any members of my family except my two sisters who were teachers and therefore expected to indulge in certain superior activities. The other was the News Theatre, which was part of the massive building which included the new City railway station and whose structure also accommodated the Queen's Hotel, a hostelry so opulent that no one I knew had ever set foot in it though it was spoken of darkly as a rendezvous for elements whose general nature was only to be revealed to me in later years. The News Theatre showed newsreels and cartoons, the former too boring and the latter too fragmentary to be of really serious interest to me.

This was far from the end of the ramifications of the distribution system. The Tower, chief cinema of another small local chain, had its own junior acolytes distributed in remote parts of the city. Inferior even to the Assembly Rooms in the Rank hierarchy was the Pavilion but, since this was on Dewsbury Road, regarded as 'rough' by my parents who had never been there but had vaguely heard of it, I was never to visit the place until much later in my cinema-going life. The Ritz, too, had its minor appendages. These were the Shaftesbury, as remote and unattainable as the Pavilion, and the Gaiety, only a few minutes' walk away once we had moved from Roundhay Road to Grange Avenue, in Chapeltown – an ascent in the social scale (no shop on the premises, four bedrooms, including two attics, for the nine of us, an indoor lavatory, and a front room never to be used in normal circumstances but suitable for receiving anxiously-awaited suitors for my sisters) which our family had achieved when I was five years old.

The Gaiety was frowned upon as being in an area as rough as the Dewsbury Road district was reputed to be, but it was near enough home to be included grudgingly among cinemas which might be visited by me. There I saw not only *The Adventures of Robin Hood* but also what I regarded as a strictly accurate historical version of *The Charge of the Light Brigade* with Errol Flynn, and Flynn again in a Western called *They Died with Their Boots On.*

Apart from Alfred and the Cakes and Bible stories, which I was told at school and believed implicitly in every detail, in my youngest years all my history lessons were taught to me via the cinema screen. It was from Warner Brothers that I learned everything I knew and everything I wanted to know about the Crimean War, wicked King John and brave King Richard. Films taught me, too, about the American Civil War (in which I found the courageous Southerners much more attractive than the sanctimonious Northerners, just as I preferred the Cavaliers to the Roundheads), Louis XIV of France (an indescribably wicked sovereign who kept his brother imprisoned in an eerie but attractive iron mask), and indeed, about British history, too, which, apart from wicked King John, brave King Richard, and the Cavaliers and the Roundheads, consisted largely of Anna Neagle being dauntingly regal, over and over again, as Queen Victoria.

The many history lessons that Greta Garbo could have taught me were all withheld, since I was never taken to any of her films, whether because they were too serious or too scandalous for me I could not discover. Similarly, I was not permitted to attend films featuring an actress of morals even more blatantly loose, who was referred to darkly as Marleen Dirty-tricks. I saw numerous Westerns, all of which I enjoyed, but none of which I could understand, since I had no idea in which country the West was situated nor in which historical period its lively happenings were set. The costumes were like none I had ever seen, the Indians were clearly some form of savage akin to those who perpetually conducted lurid sacrifices to Green Goddesses in the Tarzan films I loved, and the fact that everyone in them spoke in American accents was no reliable guide since, from what I learned from films, everybody in the whole world outside Leeds spoke in American accents apart from Queen Victoria and George Formby.

Although I was allowed to see pictures featuring Errol Flynn, I gathered that there was something wrong with him as well, from conversations about him at mealtimes which were conducted in a guarded way and with significant glances from time to time at my innocent seven-year-old head. I was of course very interested indeed in all I could find out about the performers I saw in films, and I was particularly concerned about their health since I had worked out for myself that, whenever a film was shown, those participating in it had to be present in the appropriate studio in Hollywood. Exactly how all this worked I was not very sure, since the mechanics were plainly too complicated for me to understand at present (though I was determined to get the hang of them as soon as possible). However, what was quite clear was that, if any film star – all those taking part being stars as far as I was concerned – was unwell – feeling sick, for example, as I occasionally was – then the showing of his or her movie at the Forum or Gaiety could not proceed, a disaster obviously to be avoided at all costs.

Of the technical side of films I knew nothing whatever. I knew they were photographed in some way, but how the photographs were linked together and moved was beyond me. I did not worry about how performers were able to speak since, coming as I did to films when all of them were talkies, it seemed to me quite natural that everybody involved should express themselves vocally, so much so that when eventually (from my late teens onwards) I was occasionally to see silent pictures I found them so unnatural as to be unacceptable. I have never really been able to conquer this reaction which, I am sure (and without regret) has deprived me of thousands of precious moments featuring Lillian Gish. It was also quite natural to me that films should be in black and white, since all phogographs (or 'snaps', as they were called) taken of me, such as one depicting me feeding ducks on Roundhay Park lake, were in black and white apart from some expensive oddities which were carefully hand-tinted at Charles the Photographers in Leeds (to which I had been taken to pose perplexedly beside a broken pillar). Those rare movies photographed in colour (the first I saw being a mournful Western called *The Trail of the Lonesome Pine*) were, of course, a special treat; but the over-vivid hues of the Technicolor of the mid-1930s bore no more convincing relationship to reality than the predominant and completely acceptable dun-coloured pictures which were my normal and passionately adored cinematic provender.

Films were being shown all over Leeds, in dozens of cinemas, in areas which to me, now aged ten, were unattainable and out-of-bounds. It was my firm determination to find a way of seeing as many of them as possible as soon as possible. In order to achieve this objective, I needed two important perquisites. The first was freedom of movement around the city, since the area in which I was allowed to roam was limited by the boundaries of the district in which I lived plus, eventually, 'town'. The second requirement, of course, was money. Even if permitted to travel, I needed to be able to pay the tram and bus fares (never less than ½d and sometimes as much as 2d) and of course required further funds to obtain admission to cinemas themselves, sums of money which, even at the half-price for which I qualified, generally reached 4d per visit and might even be as much as 6d. I was surrounded by the caves of Ali Baba, but the open sesame was, for the time being at any rate, denied me.

2

ESTABLISHING SHOTS

———

Emancipation came with scholastic achievement. At the age of 11, sallying forth with trepidation from Cowper Street Council School (just across from our house in Grange Avenue), I won a scholarship to Leeds Grammar School. This educational establishment was, at the time of my arrival, a direct-grant school and, with the implementation of Butler's 1944 Education Act, was to become completely independent. It had a high reputation in the city, unjustifiably so since its educational standards had been depressed by the departure to the War of all young and able-bodied masters. These were replaced in many cases by teachers who had returned from retirement to active academic service and who might be senile, dotty, vindictive, or all three at once. Most boys who went to the Grammar School were, as it was put, 'paid for', only a few dozen being scholarship boys. For a working-class boy, and a Jew into the bargain, to gain entry was regarded as something of a marvel. Accordingly, there was no doubt that to the Grammar School I would go, even though I had also won a scholarship which could have taken me to one of the High Schools administered by the Leeds City Education Department.

I found the Grammar School hard going, since there I was only one of many bright boys instead of being, as I was at Cowper Street, just about the brightest boy in the school and spoiled by always being told so. However, the school liberated me in two ways. First, I found new friends from beyond the Chapeltown area in which I lived, and some of those friends were not even Jewish. Second, Leeds Grammar was a considerable distance from where I lived and, since I had to be allowed to travel there (first by a No. 2 tram from the stop outside Cantor's fish and chip shop and then changing to the No. 1 up Woodhouse Lane), I logically must be allowed to travel equivalent distances to other remote parts of the city. Furthermore, because I needed money for tram fares and other incidental expenses, I now qualified for the receipt of regular weekly pocket money. If I used this frugally I could have a little left over for cinema tickets.

Aged 11 and a bit, I now prided myself on the fact that my film tastes were much more mature, even though I was still compelled to wear short trousers. I was moving away from Disney, who in his turn was being forced by the War to switch from cute (and, to be sure, moving) fantasies like *Dumbo* and *Bambi* to educational treatises such as *Victory Through Air Power*. My movie amusement was now provided predominantly by Abbott and Costello, on whom I doted even though I was never sure which was Abbott and which was Costello, and whom I found far funnier than the other thin and fat pair, Laurel and Hardy. The Ritz Brothers and the Three Stooges were also worth seeing. I was, however, unable to compare their humour with that of the Marx Brothers since I had never seen the Marx Brothers.

Shirley Temple dropped out of my life (she, of course, was ageing into double figures too, and as a result her film career was waning) and although my parents would have liked their beloved Deanna Durbin to replace her in my affections, I found the long songs that this plump young lady shrieked extremely boring. I was much more taken by someone called Lana Turner, whom I spotted in a very odd MGM film called *The Youngest Profession* (it was about autograph-hunters) and for whom I fell overboard when I saw her in a highly emotional movie called *Ziegfeld Girl*, in which she met tragedy through falling down dead drunk in the middle of one of the musical extravaganzas with which that film was strewn. I could not understand why such a slight and pardonable mishap should have such a damaging effect on this wonderful person's career, just as it was beyond me why Judy Garland (who had by now shed Mickey Rooney, who had turned into Andy Hardy for the duration) should, in this same film, score a fantastic success at an audition. She achieved this by singing very slowly a song called 'I'm Always Chasing Rainbows' – whose melody I much later learned was pinched from Chopin – after failing abjectly when singing it very fast, in what I personally thought was a catchy way.

I loved loud and noisy funny women, and was especially fond of the big-boned Joan Davis, the huge-mouthed Martha Raye, the totally uncontrolled Cass Daley and, most of all, Betty Hutton, who seemed to combine the best characteristics of all three (and who was briefly to become a highly effective serious actress when starred in comedies by Preston Sturges). Indeed, for Betty Hutton I broke the law. Though I had more money now than I had ever had, I still did not have very much. A band of friends and I discovered that it was possible to enter the Odeon through an imperfectly-secured exit which was conveniently located in an unfrequented side-alley. Having greatly admired Betty Hutton in *The Fleet's In*, we very much wanted to see her in a new comedy musical called *And the Angels Sing*, all the more so because it featured a pert girl with sparkling eyes by the name of Diana Lynn. One Saturday afternoon we therefore decided to enter the Odeon illicitly in order to view this film, I having established in my mind to my moral satisfaction that to go to the cinema in this way was not really a breach of the Jewish Sabbath since I would not be paying, the handing-over of money being the real sin.

We therefore crept into the cinema, and found ourselves in the darkened auditorium during the trailer. The lights went up before we had been able to sneak into vacant seats, and we were confronted by an usherette. This created panic because she was, of course, endowed with supreme authority to demand and inspect tickets which naturally we did not possess. With enormous presence of mind I boldly told this custodian, 'We're in the one-and-sixes,' and thought that she was looking at us keenly as we all made for the zone covered by that price range. There we sat, quaking as the Paramount mountain appeared on the screen and the big picture began. To one of us there then occurred a terrible thought, which he lost no time in communicating to the others: 'There are no one-and-sixes on Saturdays. They go up to one-and-nine.' With one accord the band of criminals rose and hurried to the exit through which it had entered, this time employing it for its intended purpose. It was nearly forty years before I was to see *And the Angels Sing* from beginning to end and, even though I was watching it on television in the security of my own home, I was so filled with remembered fear that I would have been unable to enjoy it even if it had turned out to be worth enjoying, which in fact it did not.

As I approached my early teens I was for some reason particularly addicted to Paramount films, possibly because they were shown at the Odeon and I loved seeing pictures at the Odeon (legally, when I could afford to pay to go in through the front entrance) because the programmes were so long. Maybe that is why I never became addicted to MGM's Red Skelton comedies but preferred not only Abbott and Costello (whose Universal films were shown at the Odeon under then-current distribution arrangements) but the 'Road' films of Bob Hope, Bing Crosby and Dorothy Lamour. These, with their allusive jokes ('Like Webster's Dictionary we're Morocco bound') seemed to me the height of sophistication, and I was beginning to regard myself as very sophisticated indeed.

When I heard Bob Hope in a sketch in *Star-Spangled Rhythm* leeringly refer to playing with his toy submarine in his bath, I thought I was terribly sharp in understanding a dirty joke. At the same time I was amazed that a Hollywood star should be involved in proceedings as vulgar as those I had been led to believe were featured in a magazine called *Razzle* which was rumoured to be very dirty indeed but of which I had no personal knowledge since I was strictly forbidden to read it. *Star-Spangled Rhythm* was one of the all-star films which Hollywood studios were churning out at the time, some of them (like *Tales of Manhattan*) being linked short stories, others (like the ineffable *Forever and a Day*) purporting to tell a coherent story, but the best, to my way of thinking, being variety shows linked by an exiguous plot.

Star-Spangled Rhythm featured popular songs like 'Hit the Road to Dreamland' and 'That Old Black Magic', but to me was most notable for a number featuring Paulette Goddard, Dorothy Lamour and Veronica Lake called 'A sweater, a sarong and a peek-a-boo bang', this title referring to the attributes by which each of these ladies was best known. The sarong, of course, belonged to Miss Lamour, whom I could never recall wearing anything else. Paulette Goddard was not the only actress noted for wearing a sweater – Lana Turner donned the garment to even greater effect, but she was under contract to MGM and so could not be included in a Paramount film – but they had to find something for her to do, and wearing a sweater was something she certainly could do. The peek-a-boo bang concealed one of the eyes of Veronica Lake, and during the performance of this number I completely ignored the sweater and the sarong and concentrated on the concealed eye, because I was hopelessly in love with Miss Lake.

I had first seen her in thrillers (very good ones, too) that she made with Alan Ladd. I later discovered that Alan Ladd was a diminutive mannikin for whom Miss Lake was the ideal co-star, since – when the scales of adoration dropped from my eyes, as sadly they did – I found out that she, too, was little taller than a dwarf. I fell for her while watching *This Gun for Hire* and *The Glass Key*, but my adoration reached its peak with *I Married a Witch*, an adaptation of a novel by Thorne Smith, which I saw over and over again until I knew almost every frame of it. Later, when I learned more about cinema as distinct from films, I found that it had been directed by René Clair and was a work of real quality; at that time I drooled over it through a haze of infatuation. My high regard for Miss Lake survived even a war film called *So Proudly We Hail*, in which, her hair pinned up to show she was taking her role as a nurse with the seriousness it required, she killed herself by embracing a hand-grenade in order to avoid disgrace at the hands of the grinning yet rapacious Japanese who populated so many American films in those days.

It was not only Veronica Lake who sang for Uncle Sam. So – in *Thank Your Lucky Stars* – did none other than Bette Davis. I was not really a fan of Miss Davis because she appeared in films too deep for me, such as *The Old Maid* and *Old Acquaintance*. She made a practice of getting the better of Miriam Hopkins, which did not in the least surprise me since I had the feeling that she could get the better of anyone through the trick she shared with my sister Gertie of breathing threateningly down her nose. True, I had gone to see her in a film in which she was not as frightening as usual, namely *Now Voyager*, during which I had cried at the moment when she took her glasses off and became a different and beautiful woman, but I was not really one for sad films either. I liked films with a happy ending, and that is why I preferred Miss Davis not only in *The Man Who Came to Dinner* (which, like the later *Sitting Pretty*, could not fail because it featured a man being rude to everyone else) but even in a comedy called *June Bride* which, I was assured by committed Davis fans, was terrible but which I enjoyed all the same. Above all, I very much approved of Miss Davis singing the somewhat rude 'They're Either Too Young Or Too Old' in *Thank Your Lucky Stars*, even though soon after seeing it I was banned for a time from going to the pictures (a truly black point in my 13-year-old life) because of an appalling school report. My parents, almost certainly accurately, ascribed this to neglect of homework in favour of sitting in darkened auditoria watching films about Occupied Europe (in which alleged and vilified collaborators with the Nazis almost always turned out to be secret resistance heroes) or Carmen Miranda behaving audaciously while wearing a good deal of fruit on her head.

The ban did not last very long, nor did it need to, because it was soon followed by a regime of self-denial imposed by none other than myself. Naturally, I read everything I could about the movies, particularly the magazines *Picturegoer* and *Picture Show*, which were not bought by any of my sisters but which I used to see at, of all places, the barber's. Our family newspaper was the *News Chronicle*, but I was not much interested in newspapers apart from the battle maps they published, since another of my interests was following the War and tracing its fortunes on huge coloured maps which were available in profusion at that time. Leafing through the *News Chronicle* after studying the war news, I came across articles about the cinema which were not simply gossip (such as that Bette Davis was a sun-worshipper, a piece of intelligence which for some considerable time left me firmly convinced that this formidable lady was a pagan who bowed down to idols) but actually expressed opinions about films, stating whether they were good or bad or something in-between, and why. I was, without at first realizing it, reading film criticism.

These articles, written by someone called Richard Winnington, came as a revelation to me. Here was someone who did not simply accept that if a film featured Veronica Lake or Bob Hope it had to be good. He examined performances and script and even direction. At that time I had no idea what a director was, and indeed, once the actors' names had appeared, regarded credit titles as a bore which had to be endured until the film's action began. I knew that, for some unexplained reason, the credit titles ended with the director's name but I did not know why, since I did not know what the director did. In fact, once the names of Lake and Hope (and of Franklin Pangborn, the pompous little man with puffy cheeks whom I thought was so funny, and of others like him such as Edward Everett Horton and the long, lanky Russian Mischa Auer) had faded from the screen, the only name I ever recognized on the credits was that of Natalie Kalmus. This indefatigable lady was always listed as in charge of the Technicolor which, it seemed, her husband either had invented or at any rate owned.

Winnington seized my attention not only because he was pungent but because he was funny and wrote memorable phrases. His review of *The Southerner* (which, without his advice, I would never have gone to see since its story was undoubtedly sad and its stars, Zachary Scott and Betty Field, were not amount my favourites) included a comment on a performance by Beulah Bond – 'It merits at least a couple of dozen Oscars at current rates' – which I not only stole myself when I became a critic, but which another much better-known critic also stole. Furthermore, Winnington accompanied his writings by deft and witty drawings which by themselves were film reviews too.

Winnington came to dominate my picture-going. To me he was not an exceptionally talented journalist who offered personal and subjective opinions but an omniscient judge who, from his chambers in Bouverie Street, delivered definitive verdicts against which there was no appeal whatsoever. I felt guilty if I saw films of which he did not approve and, since he approved of very few, I saw fewer and fewer. This was unwise of me, because while Winnington was to me then, and has been to me ever since, the nonpareil of movie critics, I eventually learned that his judgement was not flawless. He was a Marxist who judged films in very narrow political terms and he had a particularly unreasoning bias against the Hollywood system. In any case it was necessary for me to go on seeing bad pictures if I was to have any criteria by which to judge the quality of good ones. Nevertheless, my subjugation did mean that for some years my film-going was restricted. Friends became irritated with my refusal to go with them to pictures featuring stars we had previously enjoyed together. On one occasion I feigned illness in order to avoid going to an Abbott and Costello film since, at Winnington's behest, I preferred that day to see instead Noel Coward's *This Happy Breed* which my friends warned, accurately as it turned out, would be boring. So I went secretly to see *This Happy Breed* and, very fairly in the circumstances, fell ill during the performance, which did not in the least surprise my mother who had warned me against the unwise act of going to see a film in the afternoon and who, completely unsympathetic, told me that I was being punished for lying.

From time to time, by accident or force of circumstance, I saw films without Winnington's permission. I never admitted that I had enjoyed them, even if I had, since I had no authorization to obtain pleasure from them. Thus, I was permitted to enjoy *Meet Me in St Louis* because Winnington (very justly) had praised it. On the other hand, when I saw as a second feature at the Odeon a black-and-white musical which depicted dozens of girls in black stockings moving their legs in unison as piano keys, organized in the manner of Busby Berkeley and indeed possibly by Busby Berkeley, I marvelled while I was watching the stunning visual effect but then, recollecting myself, scorned what I was admiring. As a result, I have no idea of the name of this film, which I would now very much like to see again.

While the Winnington veto excluded me from many movies I might have enjoyed, the Winnington endorsement took me to films which otherwise I would never have seen, which I never failed to admire, and which sometimes gave me great pleasure. It was he who, by praising *Double Indemnity*, not only sent me to that superb *film noir* but also introduced me to the work of Billy Wilder. It was he who, in enthusing over *A Night in Casablanca*, introduced me to the Marx Brothers. Any man who sent me to see Groucho Marx justified his existence by that act alone.

It was Winnington who explained to me that the big film was not necessarily the best film, that little movies about real people, such as the American *Sunday Dinner for a Soldier* and the British *Millions Like Us*, could be more entertaining than the latest blockbuster featuring Ingrid Bergman or Gregory Peck. It was he who taught me that pictures could reveal something about life as most people lived it, without glamour or heroics, and that such movies – for example *Under The Clock*, with Judy Garland and Robert Walker, the little gem about a soldier on leave in New York and the girl he meets – could be enjoyable too.

Of course, I had to wait for a long time to see these films after I read about them. By the 1980s, except in the most unusual circumstances, a film that opened in the West End of London was shown almost simultaneously in all the main cities of the country, sometimes indeed in the few surburban cinemas that survived. Forty years earlier, the distribution system was much more ritualistic and hierarchical. A picture would run in the West End for as long as audiences could sustain it. It would then be distributed in the remainder of London, again in an ordained pattern, with the West having priority over the East, and the North over the South. Only when it had completed its first run in London would the main provincial areas have the chance to see it. Waiting for a film I very much wanted to see could be irksome, but when it finally arrived there was a sense of occasion, none more so than when *Gone with the Wind*, having run almost interminably at the Ritz, Leicester Square, was gingerly let loose in the provinces.

The queues when this much-boosted production reached the Ritz, Leeds, were so enormous, uncontrollable even, that the first time we tried to see it we failed, in the parlance of the day, to 'get in'. Turned away by the triumphantly brusque commissionaire, I left almost in tears at being deprived of a treat eagerly anticipated for so long. When at a second, successful, attempt we were eventually admitted, I was baffled by much that I saw. I remember in my puzzlement noticing my mother and my eldest sister Dora exchanging meaningful (to them, but not to me) glances as the wicked Scarlett O'Hara tore Tara's curtains down to make herself a green velvet dress. Clearly, there were mysteries in life that I was not yet equipped to penetrate.

Once a film did reach Leeds I could follow it around for months if I liked it sufficiently. For after it had been filtered through from the Odeon or Ritz or Majestic there were dozens of little tributary cinemas to which it would go, and after that it could be traced to even smaller halls in outlying villages. In the 1980s, if I miss a film I have missed it for good unless it eventually turns up on television or at the National Film Theatre. In the 1940s a movie was a feature of the local cinematic landscape for up to a year – unless, that is, it was a picture made in a foreign language, in which case I might never get the chance to see it at all.

Winnington, almost tauntingly, would often place as the lead item in his column a foreign film – that is, a film made in neither Britain nor the United States, for Hollywood movies, despite their frequently exotic and extravagant nature, were never regarded as alien. All I could then do was simply to wait and hope that it would turn up at the Tatler. When it did arrive, and even if I bought a ticket and entered the auditorium, I did not necessarily actually see the picture. This was because the Tatler had been designed by a sadist or by someone who was unaware that its purpose in existing was to display movies for public exhibition. He recognized that there would be patrons, since there was a box office, and that patrons came to the Tatler with a definite purpose, since an auditorium had been constructed purportedly as part of the amenities, and this auditorium was equipped with rows of seats. There was even a screen as well. However, the spatial relationship of the seats to the screen was such that the ability of any customer to watch a film from his seat, let alone enjoy it, was entirely coincidental.

Among the Leeds legends that adhered to the ritual of cinema-going was the one which asserted that, just as attending in the afternoon was sure to lead to head pains, so sitting in the front rows was sure to prevent a proper view of the entertainment. Nevertheless, certain people I knew deliberately chose to sit in the front. One of them, an exuberant youth called Wood, even claimed that being right at the front made him feel a participant in the proceedings, a role he ardently wished to assume, particularly when watching extravaganzas such as *The New Adventures of Don Juan*, the theme music of which (composed by the highly-regarded Max Steiner as I later discovered) he learned after a fashion to sing.

Wood was one of a group of boys with whom I used to visit the cinema regularly. The others, while certainly keen picturegoers, were not single-minded enough to qualify as addicts: they also insisted on going to cricket matches at the nearby Headingley ground (where I myself on a rare visit saw Don Bradman achieve some astronomical score) and even quite readily participated in the duties of the school's Junior Training Corps (from whose paramilitary activities I was excused on religious grounds since the Corps, as it was always curtly described, met on Saturday mornings). Wood was more artistically inclined and, for a happily brief period, tried to learn the violin under the tuition of an earnest but despairing instructor by the name of Walter Jorytz.

It was with Wood that I laughed in a superior manner when our hated headmaster, Dr Terry Thomas, announced at assembly that the next lunchtime concert in Upper School would feature the Farquharson Cousins; we both knew that these promised entertainers were not a close-harmony group but, in fact, one person, namely the principal French horn of the Yorkshire Symphony Orchestra. It was with Wood that I organized the unofficial, indeed clandestine, Leeds Grammar School Festival of Music and Drama. This featured the world première (and, as it turned out, dernière) of a sonata composed especially for the occasion by a boy called Collick who was a precocious admirer of an almost unknown composer named Josef Holbrooke and who, for unfathomable reasons, adopted the soubriquet of Robert Anton for this sole occasion.

Wood was always reliable as a cinema companion because he was ready to go to absolutely anything. Not even he, however, wanted to sit in one of the front rows at the Tatler. Not only were they so near the screen as to be practically behind it; in addition, the seats at the side stretched so far into the distance as to distort almost beyond recognition the images at which the desperate viewer frantically squinted. These inferior seats, being the cheapest, were the only ones we could afford. Nevertheless, despite these daunting handicaps, we went to the Tatler, Wood humouring me simply because he was bold enough to confront any circumstances, however adverse or challenging.

Winnington certainly recommended some oddities, since his politics imbued in him a peculiar regard for Soviet films which, if they had been made in any other country, he would have dismissed as cumbersome propaganda. Moreover, scorning the admittedly vivid Technicolor hues over which Mrs Kalmus solicitously presided, he praised the Russian process of Sovcolor as being far more verisimilitudinous. Wood, who liked everything in films, including colour, to be more heightened than in real life, denounced Sovcolor as insipid. I argued with him, since to me Winnington's word was law, but secretly admitted to myself that Wood did have a point. In fact, Sovcolor was drab and dispiriting, rather like the horrible Trucolor by Consolidated featured in films made by the poverty-stricken Republic studios which was later to infest our screens together with Anscocolor, Eastman Color, Warnercolor, Metrocolor, Cinecolor, Supercinecolor, Color by De Luxe and all the other processes which came into vogue as Mrs Kalmus gradually relaxed her iron grip.

However, while watching Stalin benevolently presiding over the frolics of little Russian children was neither intellectually stimulating nor, it had to be conceded, in any way entertaining, films directed by Jean Cocteau, Julien Duvivier, Marcel Carné and René Clair were both. The revelations of Jean Gabin in *Le Jour Se Lève*, and of the gorgeous Arletty in that film and in *Les Enfants du Paradis* and *Les Visiteurs du Soir*, were worth all the agonies of attendance at the Tatler – even though I only managed to see parts of them because of the distortion experienced in the side seats at the front and because a large percentage of my time at the Tatler was spent not in watching the screen but in gazing frantically around the auditorium desperately hoping that someone in a better seat would leave. Should such an opportunity occur, I would immediately dart out of my own seat, in vicious competition with others involved in the same pursuit. In such a situation it was each cinemagoer for himself, with pushing and elbowing recognized as tactics justifiably to be employed. For losers there was the penalty of quite possibly finding, when one slunk back to one's own seat in defeat, that this in its turn had been claimed by someone who had been even worse situated, who would in no circumstances be willing to surrender his present place. At that point there was no choice but to stand at the side, though of course even that humiliating and unsatisfactory position depended on the rather fragile goodwill of the usherette, who naturally felt that her own arbitrary allocation of seats should have settled the matter in the first place.

At the Tatler I also encountered for the first time the phenomena of subtitles and dubbing. My knowledge of French was limited, as would have been that of anyone whose acquisition of the language was supervised by the rather decrepit teaching staff at Leeds Grammar School. My knowledge of Russian, of Spanish (spoken in some of the Buñuel films which were to follow), of Danish (the language of Carl Dreyer's horrific *Vredensdag*) and of all other languages except classical Greek and Latin was non-existent. The distributors of foreign-language films, then as now, catered for this ignorance by translation of the dialogue. Both subtitling and dubbing appeared to me on first encounter to be unsatisfactory and both have proved so ever since.

The manufacturers of the subtitles seemed to have a cavalier approach to their duties. Accurate translation was not necessarily their objective. Whatever else *Sait-On Jamais?* means, it does not mean *No Sun in Venice*. By mistake I saw *Knave of Hearts* twice, once when it was exhibited under that title, again when shown under its French name *Monsieur Ripois*. So depressing did I find it (like most other works directed by René Clement) that I would have preferred not to have seen it at all. Again, the nature of the translation of dialogue was disconcerting. Enormously long speeches might be transmogrified into three words in the subtitles. Conversely, a curt remark might achieve a translation that covered all the lower half of the screen. I was later to find when cinema-going in Israel that the subtitles there always did cover the lower half of the screen, since the authorities in that country, no doubt for pressing reasons, had a practice of providing subtitles in two languages, Hebrew and one other.

Necessary as some form of translation was, subtitling distracted the attention from the images I had come to observe. The eye switched from the action to the printed words and back again. These irritations, however, did not compare with those imposed by dubbing. In theory, to listen to the characters speaking English should have enabled me to concentrate on plot and camerawork. Far from it. I spent my time carefully watching the mouths of the speakers, seeking to note to what extent the contortions of their lips matched the words apparently issuing from them. I noted that they never did, quite. Despite the efforts of the dubbers to provide spoken words in English that lasted precisely as long as the visual evidence of speech, there was always a little overlap during which the actor silently mouthed a syllable. Furthermore, the syllables did not always match. A screen 'o' might be paralleled by a soundtrack 'i', and the results were incongruous. Even more incongruous, however, were the voices used. Anna Magnani, howling her head off in some purportedly accurate depiction of a lively Italian discussion, would be given the voice of a prim young lady brought up in deepest Kensington. A comic character in an Italian film would, in an attempt at a British counterpart, be given a Cockney accent which did not suit at all. The experience was extremely disconcerting to all except those utterly determined to be entertained or edified whatever the handicaps.

I was one of those with the necessary determination. Secretly, I much preferred films originally made with English dialogue. Moreover, my predilection for films without sad endings covertly persisted. Unlike Wood, who flaunted these tastes, I did not dare to admit to mine in case Winnington should in some way find out. So, while Wood went off unashamedly to see spectacles, epics, comedies and musicals, I stuck it out at the Tatler, suffering with the bicycle thieves, watching witches burnt at the stake in the most harrowing circumstances, hiding my head while legless cripples went through indescribable sufferings, moaning as lovers suffered agonies of parting prior to one of them being guillotined, flinching at lacerations and injections – forcing myself to watch physical and psychological degradation and pretending all the while that I was enjoying myself.

Of course, some of the films I certainly did enjoy. I came to love Michel Simon (whose face seemed to consist of potatoes of various sizes stuck together) especially for his performance in Carné's almost unique comedy, *Drôle de Drame*. While I flinched at de Sica's more depressing masterworks, I rejoiced in his magnificently funny *Miracle in Milan*. If I soon tired of Fernandel when he stopped bothering to act and instead simply exploited his superbly grotesque face, I relished him while he was still acting, for example in the early comedy *Fric Frac*.

Moreover, even when I was suffering I was learning. My diet of French pictures may have been limited to pre-war and wartime films in which Carné, Duvivier and Cocteau predominated disproportionately; my knowledge of Italy was based on Vittorio de Sica and Roberto Rossellini. Yet these directors were involved in the production of great masterpieces and, even handicapped as I was by my limited adolescent appreciation, I did have the chance to see how atmosphere was created by lighting and editing and camera movement, and had the opportunity, at an age when my ability to make judgements was being formed, to see some of the greatest performances that were ever to be filmed. My knowledge of Hollywood's past remained almost nil, and that of Hollywood's present was constricted by deliberate self-deprivation. I was, however, slowly and without any judgement, obtaining some sort of grounding in the products of international cinema.

The 16-year-old youth who sat in the Tatler, peering anxiously at the screen with feelings of fear, repulsion or bafflement, was undoubtedly a snob and a prig; but his horizons were widening.

3

TRAVELLING MATTE

_____

What I needed now was liberation. Not financial liberation, for I was being given money by my father and, in any case, the cheapest cinema seats did not cost very much; nor geographical liberation because, in my mid-teens, I was free to go where I liked and public transport was available to take me there. No. I needed intellectual liberation, if the word 'intellectual' could be applied to the mental activities of a youth whose pretensions far exceeded his knowledge. I needed to be freed from the shackles of Winnington's judgements.

My emancipation came swiftly. First, visiting the cinema was becoming at any rate in part a social affair, though one girl I went with expressed some perplexity that I spent so much of my time with her in the dark taking notes. Second, my appetite for films was now so insatiable that it simply could not be slaked on the meagre rations permitted by my mentor from the _News Chronicle_. So, although I turned up my nose at a lot of what I saw (while enjoying it all the same), I saw a very great deal.

My viewing of films required careful planning. Both of the local newspapers had to be studied, since some cinemas advertised in one but not the other. We had delivered to us at home the _Yorkshire Evening Post_, a newspaper owned by the Yorkshire Conservative Newspaper Company. It published strong leading articles on the merits of corporal punishment and, for reasons I was never able to understand, was somehow regarded as more respectable than the _Yorkshire Evening News_. Apart from the aforementioned leading articles and the omission from the _News_ of a _Post_ regular feature entitled 'Yorkshire Conservative Diary', providing information about genteel but vengeful whist drives and garden parties organized for those who inexplicably did not wish to go to the cinema, both newspapers seemed to have nearly identical contents. These consisted of news items about various disasters afflicting people who lived in Yorkshire, or who had done so at some point in the past, who had visited Yorkshire for

42

however brief a period, or who had intended at some point in their lives to visit Yorkshire. To the *Post* and the *News* their favourite member of the Royal Family was the Princess Royal, who had demonstrated an undeniably good sense by choosing Harewood House in Yorkshire as her residence.

The *News*, therefore, had to be bought out of my own pocket or, if my financial circumstances were straitened as they quite often were, studied in the reading room either of the local Sheepscar Library (where the meticulous clerks compelled juvenile patrons to wash their hands before fingering any of the stock) or else at the Central Library. The Central, round the corner from Leeds's one wartime architectural casualty, the City Museum, was always interesting since it was much frequented by shabby, unshaven and to be perfectly blunt – absolutely filthy men who used this warm room as a shelter before nipping out for the methylated spirits that was reputed to be their principal, indeed possibly sole, sustenance. There was, however, always a risk of disappointment in venturing into the Central Library, since it was possible that one of these men might have fallen asleep (a state almost certainly induced by the methylated spirits) over the *Evening News*, a situation which would of course have confirmed my parents in their conviction that the *Post* was the more respectable of the two.

If I wanted to arrange to see all the films that attracted me, planning of almost military precision was required, with graph paper an aid not to be despised. Outside the centre of the city, almost all cinemas offered two main programmes a week, one from Monday to Wednesday, the other from Thursday to Saturday. Certain others in less socially elevated areas went so far as to provide three programmes a week, each being shown on two days. In addition, picture houses which availed themselves of the right to Sunday opening (a boon conferred on Leeds as a result of a referendum held in 1946, in which I canvassed with much more commitment than in the previous year's general election) were required to have an entirely different programme on that day presumably as some kind of penitence for competing with church services although, to limit such a clash, cinemas' hours of opening on Sundays were restricted. Almost all of these multifarious programmes consisted of two films each. These arrangements meant that during any given week several hundred films were available for view in Leeds, and the choice was frequently tormenting. That choice was even greater than seemed apparent from study of the press because some cinemas, to make matters more confusing, advertised in neither newspaper, instead providing details in tiny print on posters which I earnestly studied on a hoarding in a deserted street not too far from the Central railway station.

The quality of the films available was, of course, a major fact in selection of venue. So too, however, was length of programme, which could be judged from timings cited in the newspaper advertisements. These, although they often did not give the hour of commencement of each picture, always provided Delphic information about what was called 'LCP'. These mystic capital letters, which needed no explanation whatever to addicts, stood for 'Last Complete Programme', and, naturally, the earlier the time printed next to LCP, the longer the programme and the greater the value for money.

Distance to be travelled was critical; but so was location. Dependence on buses (the trams having been abolished, or sold to Blackpool, in a misguided outburst of modernity) involved delicate logistics. Those of us who were going to the pictures would meet in town at the information kiosk in City Square. (This kiosk, a facility made available by Leeds City Transport Department, theoretically was available to provide information about bus services. It was rarely open at any hour. Eventually it was closed down and was soon after demolished. Nevertheless we continued to meet at its site.) However we obtained the information, it was essential for us to know what time the last bus left from our destined cinema. If necessary we could walk home from town, since that was not far, but if we were setting out to somewhere new we could not risk missing the last bus as the distance home might be too far for us to walk.

The nature of the cinema to be visited also had to be considered. If the chosen film was of so compelling a nature that all other arguments fell before the necessity of viewing it, that was that. Otherwise, it had to be faced that certain cinemas could be patronized only if absolutely nothing worth seeing was showing anywhere else. In our circle small cinemas were generically described as fleapits or bug-hutches; certain of them, however, did indeed harbour noxious insects or were so dirty or decrepit that the possibility of catching some disease in them could not be ruled out. The Newtown picture house, quite close to where I lived, was as near out-of-bounds as any cinema could be to us, even though it cost only 2d. to get in. Some cinemas smelled very heavily indeed of disinfectant; this, on the whole, was regarded as a good sign though cinematically it was no substitute for the brief, unsuccessful experiment with Smell-O-Vision which was attempted some years later.

In addition, we had to consider the kind of audience that a given cinema attracted. It was not that we were afraid of any loutish elements who might frequent a particular picture house. Indeed I can claim with pride that I have never suffered violence at any cinema I have visited anywhere in the world, much as from time to time I might have deserved it. However, experience taught us that there were some places where the audience went certainly to watch the film but also to indulge in rowdiness which, on occasion, could verge on riot. Naturally their din interfered with enjoyment of what was being projected on to the screen. Hushings did no good. Our fellow-patrons, being entirely unaware that what they were doing was anything out of the ordinary or called for comment or restraint, did not know that such hushings were directed at them – if, that is, they could even hear our remonstrations.

To try to cope with such manifestations, some cinemas employed not only usherettes but invigilators, whose duty was to move constantly among the audience attempting to maintain discipline. These were generally sour, lowering men, often of advanced age, and their appearance did sometimes halt certain patently unsocial activities such as rolling bottles down aisles (this being before the age of canned or packeted beverages). One such functionary, in a cinema in the district of Holbeck, was armed with a pole long enough to reach to the middle of any row, so that every miscreant in the auditorium was within range of his admonitions. He patrolled the aisles, equipped with a huge torch whose beam was so powerful that it could have been employed to illuminate night-time football matches. In the event of some transgression being revealed by his searchlight, with commendable accuracy he would probe the pole along the row until it made contact with the culprit, who might well be the object of quite a sharp dig. The problem with this invigilator was that he was completely undiscriminating in his attentions. He not only might direct them at members of the audience who were offering audible advice to the participants in the screen drama or who were fighting among

themselves; he could also take unreasonable exception to sophisticated comments of criticism or appreciation which were being
offered, slightly above our breaths, by my companions and myself.

The name of a cinema was not necessarily a guide to its quality.
Suburban picture houses, not always of the most salubrious kind,
included a Gainsborough, a Grosvenor, an Imperial, a Savoy, and
no fewer than three Palaces. The Palace, Holbeck, was especially
misnamed, consisting as it did of a kind of hut into which rain
seemed to leak even when it was not falling outside. Some
cinemas – the Newtown being one and the Victory, near to which
a murder had been committed, most certainly another – were to
be visited only in the rarest of circumstances. On the other hand,
the names of some picture houses, when attached to the districts
in which they were located, were redolent with a romanticism
which attracted us even when the films they were showing were
not of the choicest. These included the Lyric, Tong Road, the
Regent, Burmantofts, the Tivoli, Middleton, and, above all, the
Western, Florence Street, which as it happened was also a kind of
hut, though relatively rainproof.

Not surprisingly, the snobby areas had the best picture houses.
The Kingsway in Moortown (companion to the Clock) was very
genteel and, indeed, of so sanctified a nature that it came as no
surprise when the Jewish community purchased it and turned it
into a synagogue (the men sitting in what used to be the stalls,
while the women were relegated to what used to be the best seats,
in the circle) – a rather more respectable fate than struck many
cinemas which ended up as bingo halls if they were not demolished
altogether. This was a synagogue at which I eventually, and
entirely appropriately, worshipped, though it did seem odd to be
fasting on Yom Kippur in approximately the same spot where I
had shivered in fear during some of the tensest moments of *A
Woman's Face*, starring Joan Crawford at her most transcendental.

Moortown was at any rate on the No. 2 bus route, and could be
reached quite conveniently from my home in Chapeltown. En
route was the Dominion, in Chapel Allerton, much favoured until
a harsh fate struck and burned it down. Rebuilt and re-opened for
business amid appropriate celebrations, it failed commercially
and was turned into a bingo hall. Dozens of others, lamentably,
also disappeared, some demolished, some consigned to bingo,
others used as business premises or offices, others replaced by
housing. The Clifton, Bramley, became a do-it-yourself centre,

Moortown Corner House (which for a time instituted an unheard-of and doomed policy of not admitting customers after the big picture had started), a casino. The Gaiety was replaced by a pub, and the Gainsborough a warehouse (as was the Newtown too, though this was not, I trust, a building housing perishable goods). The Pavilion, Dewsbury Road, became a warehouse as well, the Pavilion, Stanningley, a car showroom, and the site of the Regal, Crossgates, possibly the most attractive and luxurious of all the suburban cinemas, was used for a supermarket.

Thirty-five years and more ago all of these were flourishing. Many would often have queues outside when we arrived there. Our group of adolescent *cinéastes* would set off into the unknown, asking the bus conductor to give us a shout when we got to the stop nearest to our destination. Some conductors actually remembered to do so, but to make sure of not missing our stop we would also ask advice from various passengers, most of whom had never heard of where we were going and many of whom thought we were mad for going there whether they knew where it was or not. Sometimes we would mistakenly leave the bus either long before we reached our destination or far beyond it, and would than have to intercept pedestrians to ask the way. These, too, looked at us askance, either because they did not understand what we were talking about or because they thought we looked dangerous.

Eventually we would arrive, to enjoy the mystery and possibly the pleasure of a cinema we had never seen before. Some of these new discoveries would be huge, others tiny, some gleaming, others dingy. Some would have stalls and a circle, others all their seats on the ground floor or even in the basement. Some would be long, tunnel-like structures, with the screen almost invisibly distant from the back rows. Some would have projection equipment with lights so weak that the image was so dim as to be almost imperceptible. Others would have sound equipment so faulty that it was almost impossible to hear anything said, even if there was no hubbub from the audience. Others still – or possibly the same ones – would have screens that were torn or stained or partly obscured by untidily drawn curtains. Others again would have mis-shapen or foreshortened screens, so that part of the image would be projected on to the walls, the ceiling or even the floor. We would debate where to sit, resisting the attempts by the usherette to break us up into manageable numbers (if there were many of us) or to put us in seats right at the side or right at the front. While organized and syndicated advertisements had not yet become common, slides advertising local furniture shops or hairdressers would give us a sample of life in the area.

Eventually, Leeds itself proved too small for us, and we began venturing first into neighbouring villages and then to nearby townships and towns. We would go out to Horsforth and Guiseley in the wool area, and to mining villages like Glasshoughton whose local cinema, surprisingly named the Cosy, was situated on what seemed to be a piece of wasteland but showed remarkably enterprising programmes. We went out to Bradford, where a picture house dishonestly called the Elite, situated up a steep hill, often showed films we wanted to see, and then, more ambitiously, to Wakefield, to Dewsbury, to Doncaster. One of our number bought a motorcycle and we would take it in turns to ride pillion, careering through the dark, cold, windy and wet night to tumble, on our return to Leeds, into one of the pubs near City Square to get warm.

We traversed Yorkshire, or at any rate the West Riding. It was scarcely the West Riding of the dales and moors, though we saw a good deal of those out of the grimy windows of the West Yorkshire Road Car's buses and from dingy little trains trundling through tiny stone-built stations all of which seemed to be called 'Virol'. We did, however, see a Yorkshire as real as any, an urban Yorkshire, an industrial Yorkshire, a working-class Yorkshire, since the cinemas we visited were mostly in manufacturing towns. We saw cobbled alleys and factory chimneys and back-to-back houses and streets lit by gas lamps. In pursuit of an artificial world, we blundered into a real world that we might otherwise never have noticed.

Regardless of the films we saw, going to the pictures certainly broadened our minds. For rare and very special occasions moviegoing even took us across the Pennines to Manchester, to sit in cinemas so large and opulent that they were thought to compare with the fabled picture palaces in the West End of London which none of us, of course, had ever visited, but where it was rumoured that it cost as much as 3s.6d. to go in.

My parents, who had lived there for more than thirty years, had never been to most of the areas of Leeds to which I now went habitually. They thought there was something eccentric, or even worse, about me that sent me to places like Wortley and Beeston – as remote to them as the far side of the moon – to see films, when there were films to be seen, even if not the same films, but a film was a film, right there in Chapeltown. If my school work had suffered they might well have tried to stop me, but I had rehabilitated myself after the total negligence which had resulted in that appalling report and was now doing pretty well: in fact, to be frank, very well. So they muttered and murmured, but by the time I started going as far as Manchester they recognized that I was incorrigible. I was afflicted with a mania, and that was that.

So off I went, and my appetite grew on what it fed on. Compromise with my friends meant that I would go to films that others favoured in return for their coming to something that I particularly wanted to see. So I got to know the work of Robert Hamer and became an admirer of not only the heartless black comedy *Kind Hearts and Coronets* but of the realistic melodrama *It Always Rains on Sunday* too. I saw *Madame Bovary* and was intoxicated by its swirling waltz scene without realizing that this bravura episode was characteristic of its director, Vincente Minnelli – of whom, in fact, I had never heard at that time. I had the good sense to recognize that the adventure movie *The Crimson Pirate* was a work of wit and quality, but that the apparently similar *The Flame and the Arrow*, also featuring Burt Lancaster, was not. Veronica Lake having been cast ruthlessly aside, I was infatuated with a series of English actresses, most notably Joan Greenwood (hoarsely cooing 'Looo-ie' as she led the hero-murderer to his doom in *Kind Hearts and Coronets*).

I saw the pacifist film *The Boy with Green Hair* and knew there was something pretentious about it and about its director, Joseph Losey, whom I confused with Joseph Pevney; but I shed tears over *Little Women* even though it contained June Allyson at her most gruesome (and miscast). I saw the Marx Brothers' worst film, *Love Happy*, without noticing that the smallest role, Brunion's client, was played by one Marilyn Monroe. As a result of strenuous efforts, I avoided seeing *The Jolson Story* (and indeed I have never seen it). The years, filled with a delicious mélange of films good and bad, went by. I reached my early twenties and then, despite strenuous efforts to avoid the experience, I was dragged reluctantly along to see *Singin' in the Rain*.

4

MUSIC TRACK

———

Since *The Three Little Pigs*, I had of course seen many musicals. I had, however, been to very few specifically because they were musicals and to very many despite their being musicals. Naturally, at an early age I had gone to see *The Wizard of Oz*, because it was a children's film, but I had regarded 'Over the Rainbow' as a sloppy song that held up the action and delayed the switch from boring black and white to exciting colour when Dorothy arrived in Oz. If I was to consider as memorable any number from this movie it would have been either 'We're off to see the Wizard' (whose music was published in the *News of the World* and which I learned to play with one finger on the Schubert piano in the forbidden zone of our front room) or 'We Represent the Lollipop Guild', sung by a group of winsome Munchkins (who, I learned much later, were an uncontrollable band of drunken sex-maniacs whose behaviour as a kind of midget Hitler Youth helped drive Victor Fleming away from the Oz set to direct *Gone with the Wind*).

I saw other films in which July Garland sang, but if I enjoyed them it was because they were about young people who were initially thwarted by hostile adults but then won them over – all except the nasty ones, who often seemed to include (wearing modern dress) Margaret Hamilton, the baneful lady with the long face who played the Wicked Witch of the West in *The Wizard of Oz*. I also saw many of the adventures of another young girl who sang, Deanna Durbin (who, as it happened, was MGM's first choice for Dorothy but happily could not be obtained from the studios, Universal, who owned her). I enjoyed these much less, first because I thought Miss Durbin was too fat and second because she sang in a high screaming voice which seemed to please adults but as far as I was concerned simply interrupted the plot, such as it was, of the rather prissy films in which she spent her time fussily winning over curmudgeonly older persons.

I could just about tolerate Judy Garland in *Little Nelly Kelly*

50

because, while she started out singing slow songs and then cast a gloom over things by dying, she was reincarnated as a young American girl who sang quick songs (like 'It's a Great Day for the Irish') while marching along Fifth Avenue, which seemed to be the Briggate of New York. Richard Winnington had permitted me to see her in *Meet Me in St Louis* but, despite the merry 'Trolley Song', I liked this film best for the comedy provided by such characters as the redoubtable Marjorie Main. By the time I saw Garland in *For Me and My Gal* I was off her completely, since I thought the film depressing and unpleasant, not least because of a disagreeable character played by an actor I had not seen before, Gene Kelly, who, in a scene that made me wince, deliberately maimed himself to avoid serving in the US forces in the First World War. At the time of their release I saw none of the major films that Judy Garland made for MGM; I know them all well now, but only because I managed to seek them out in revival halls.

I had been to various other musicals, wartime patriotic farragos in which famous classical performers like Jose Iturbi would descend to the level of the common man, grinning away in paroxysms of bonhomie while banging or plucking away in some anti-Nazi finale of stupefying tastelessness. One of these (in *Thousands Cheer*), was, astoundingly, especially composed for MGM by Shostakovich. On the whole, though, musicals comprised a very small proportion of the films that I saw, since generally I deliberately kept away from them.

For one thing, I was baffled by the way in which some of the numbers were presented. The camera would show members of a theatre audience, usually sitting in a box (and alienating me right away, since it was impossible for me to identify with people as rich as that), and then there would be a cut to a page of a programme naming a song that was about to be performed. I got the impression that American musical stage shows consisted of dozens of unconnected items separated by the curtain going up and down, which must have made for a long evening, to which I had no objection in principle provided the shows were not boring, a proviso cancelled by what happened next. Up would go the curtain. There would be a cut to the people in the box applauding (nice and economical in reducing the number of extras who were required) and then, on to the stage would walk a singer who would start to intone the words of the number the programme had announced. This would go on for a minute or two, and then the singer would walk towards the back of the stage, which would expand far beyond the space available on any stage in the history of the world. Dancers would appear, dozens, possibly hundreds, and frolic among mountains or in clouds that could certainly not be accommodated within a theatre. There would be overhead views, and angles achieved from beneath and sometimes through glass or even mirrors. Mist would envelop what we were being shown and then disperse to reveal some other elaborate scene, a jungle perhaps, or the Scottish Highlands. Countless new performers, garbed differently and extravagantly, would then appear and cavort. All this while the original song was going on but with different rhythms and novel orchestration, and possibly shrieked by an invisible heavenly chorus. After these implausible events had gone on for some considerable time, there would be a cut back to the original singer standing at the side of the stage, who would finish alone what he or she had started alone. The people in the box, who could not possibly have seen all, if indeed any, of this, would applaud enthusiastically, turning to each other and smiling and nodding the while, and the curtain would then fall. Logic told me that what I had seen was impossible, that the laws of time and space had been intolerably violated, but apparently no one but me seemed to mind or even notice. I rejected the whole procedure as making no kind of sense, quite apart from the consideration that most if not all of what I had seen bored me out of my wits.

I had never seen any of the musicals co-starring Fred Astaire and Ginger Rogers. I had heard about them of course; my sisters avidly went to see them, and returned home trying to remember the words of songs such as 'The Continental'. From what they said, however, I did not fancy these pictures: simply a man and woman (he, from stills I looked at outside cinemas, wearing clothes I had only seen worn by bridegrooms at Jewish weddings, she for some reason garbed in a nightie) dancing about and no doubt holding up whatever story there was, if indeed there was much of one at all. I would probably have tried one or two if I had known about the contributions to them of Edward Everett Horton and Eric Blore since, as in the case of Franklin Pangborn, I was much addicted to these players of minor comic roles. The only time I recall having seen Fred Astaire was in Paramount's *Holiday Inn*, the film which launched the song 'White Christmas' upon an

unoffending world. Ginger Rogers I had enjoyed at the Kingsway
in its pre-synagogue days, in a comedy called *Bachelor Mother*, the
implications of its title being at the time far beyond my comprehension. She seemed quite a cheery soul, and I was perfectly
prepared to watch her in other films if she could really justify my
attendance. She was not, however, likely to do so by dancing
about, with Astaire or with anyone else.

So when a friend tried to persuade me to go with him to a new
film at the Ritz, I resisted. The friend's name was Speakman, and
he was a chemistry student who seemed to me to be incredibly
brainy because he had deep knowledge of things called polymers,
which expertise enabled him to explain to me the scientific
principles underlying the plot of *The Man in the White Suit*, a
melancholy comedy starring Alec Guinness as a guileless inventor
thwarted at every turn by vested interests. Even more profound
was Speakman's devotion – brief in each case, but truly serious
while it lasted – to a succession of young actresses, in his passion
for whose burgeoning careers he attempted to enmesh me. Badgered
by him, I had sat through *The Secret People* and *The Clouded
Yellow* while he gazed soulfully at their respective stars, an
adolescent Audrey Hepburn and a similarly gawky Jean Simmons.
Now there was a new one he wanted me to have a look at, and she
was performing in, of all things, a musical. This particular picture
he nagged me to attend sounded tedious and old-fashioned, based
on a song which I had vaguely known for ages and did not
especially like. I had heard of no one in it apart from Donald
O'Connor, whom I had seen in the first of a banal movie series
about a talking mule, and Gene Kelly, whom I had not much
cared for in *For Me and My Gal*, although I had quite enjoyed *On
the Town* because Richard Winnington told me to like it and
because I fell for Ann Miller doing her 'Prehistoric Man' number
in a museum full of animal skeletons. In the end I went, because I
could not propose any more attractive alternative and because
going to any picture was better than going to none; but I went
with very little hope of pleasure to come.

Singin' in the Rain did not open very promisingly; the credit
titles were dull and the songs played over them were familiar
without being pleasantly nostalgic. There was quite a funny scene
at the beginning outside a Hollywood film première, followed by
what I had to concede was an entertaining flashback sequence.
When, behind the scenes at the movie-house, the silent-picture

actress Lina Lamont burst into shrill abuse I laughed quite a lot, but nevertheless regarded the characterization as a crib from the voice Judy Holliday used in *Born Yesterday*. Then came a party sequence. People stood around. A huge cake was wheeled in. A few bars of music were played, a kind of little fanfare. Then, suddenly, there burst out of this cake a gorgeous girl dressed in pink. This was my first sight ever of Debbie Reynolds, 19 years old and blooming with life. She was the actress whom Speakman had wanted to inspect. Joined by other girls similarly clad, she began to dance to a tune called 'All I Do is Dream of You'. A huge smile broke over my face; I was utterly captivated. I became more and more entranced as the film went on, with its extraordinary sequences (the best, I thought then, being Kelly and O'Connor tap-dancing to tongue-twisters in 'Moses Supposes'), its sharp comedy, its precision camera movement and, of course, the title number with Kelly literally singing and dancing in the rain, splashing in puddles for sheer joy, like a child. I had never seen a film that employed and combined acting, singing, dancing, set decoration, soundtrack, camera movement and editing in such a bewitching way.

By the 1980s, of course, *Singin' in the Rain* had come to be regarded as one of the greatest classics of the cinema, included in lists of the Ten Best alongside *The Battleship Potemkin* and *Citizen Kane*. When I saw it, in Leeds in 1952, it was just another film, made at a modest cost to be exhibited for a week to as many people as would be willing to pay and then to be consigned to the graveyard of routine movies, with no widespread television networks or videotapes to revive it, no future foreseeable except just possibly on 16 mm to be shown by amateurs. For me, however, it was a major, even a crucial, event in my life, comparable to the evening when I first saw *The Marriage of Figaro* and the music of Mozart became a paramount part of my consciousness.

My family had for years regarded my propensity to see certain films more than once as something of an eccentricity. That eccentricity now became a mania. I could not wait to see *Singin' in the Rain* again – and again, and again, and again. I followed it all round Leeds, all around Yorkshire, from township to township. I came to know its screenplay almost word for word. I could summon up in my mind practically each individual shot and relished them all, even those to which I had paid no attention on my first viewing. With a care appropriate to performances by

Irving or Bernhardt, I scrutinized minor characters playing tiny parts – Douglas Fowley as the exasperated director of the film within the film, Kathleen Freeman as Phoebe Dinsmore, the maddeningly meticulous diction instructress. I saw the film twenty-one times and then gave up counting; I did not, however, give up seeing it. I was the victim of an *amour fou* for a piece of celluloid.

Having been captured by *Singin' in the Rain* I could not wait to see more musicals. I knew instinctively – and, as it turned out, rightly – that there could never again be anything either like it or as good as it. This one film had, however, definitively broken down my prejudices against musicals as a species of film, and I now went to as many as I could in the hope of repeating to some degree part of the pleasure I had obtained from it.

I soon found that most musicals remained as bad as I had previously thought all musicals were. *Singin' in the Rain* was, of course, produced at MGM studios in Culver City, Los Angeles, and accordingly I had less high hopes of the products of other studios. I found that at the start of the 1950s each of these rival film establishments had discernible individual styles for films manufactured to their own particular formulae.

I learned that Twentieth Century-Fox concentrated on back-stage musicals, and these proved almost universally dire. The songs were performed on-stage and interrupted the action, rather than off-stage and as part of the action, as in *Singin' in the Rain*. First there would be a chunk of plot, featuring one of Fox's Identikit heroes such as John Payne or, later, Dale Robertson. (At quite an early age I realized that most films contained either a top male star or a top female star, with the chief protagonist of the other sex being a faceless make-weight.) The job of these men was to sulk before being won over – or not, as the case might just occasionally be – by the good nature of the star, usually Alice Faye or Betty Grable. Then all development of the story ground to a halt while a static number was performed, with reaction shots from the auditorium or the wings. I was soon in a position to write a screen treatment for a Fox musical which would have been indistinguishable from, and in no way inferior to, the themes of such dreary products as *Wabash Avenue, Tin Pan Alley, My Blue Heaven* and *Meet Me after the Show*.

Fox musicals looked up a bit when Grable was superseded by someone with a bit more life, the Marilyn Monroe I had failed to notice in *Love Happy*. While in her dramatic films (such as *Don't Bother to Knock* and *Niagara*) Miss Monroe was required to pout and maybe commit murder a bit, in her musicals she was only required to impersonate a good-natured imbecile, which seemed well within her range. So the mood of Fox musicals changed, on the whole, from ill-temper to good nature, though in *There's No Business like Show Business* there was a mixture of the two. This film, however, was worth it because of the consecration of Johnnie Ray, the crying crooner, into the priesthood.

I was beginning to understand that the quality of the script and direction could have an effect on a performance. Previously I had had some kind of idea that performers went into a studio and made up what they said and did as they went along. Now I realized that an actor was only as good as what he or she was given to do. In *Singin' in the Rain* Donald O'Connor (of whom I had previously not had much of an opinion, on the whole preferring the performance of Francis the talking mule in their scenes together) had astounded me by his terrific tap-dancing in 'Moses Supposes' and 'Good Morning' and, of course, in his almost super-human 'Make 'Em Laugh' number, in which he made love to a tailor's dummy and danced upwards on a wall until he was upside-down. In Fox's *Call Me Madam* (as well as *There's No Business like Show Business*) nobody thought up anything in particular for him, so he just stood around being complacent.

Warner Brothers, too, went in for ill-tempered musicals in which people quarrelled a good deal before making up at the last possible moment. They also seemed to find it almost impossible to get anyone to write new songs for them, and the very titles of Warner Brothers' films were enough to put me off, consisting predominantly of the names of tunes I was used to hearing my mother humming in the kitchen while making the chicken soup. Honestly, who wanted to go to see pictures with titles like *Lullaby of Broadway*, *On Moonlight Bay*, *April in Paris*, and *By the Light of the Silvery Moon*? Into the bargain, it was almost certain that you were going to get Doris Day singing any or all of these numbers, and who wanted to watch that sexless doll standing at the left of the screen, facing rightwards in profile, possibly dappled with a little moonlight, soulfully intoning numbers that were not enlivened by any originality or invention? I later discovered that I was being unfair to Miss Day, because in the musical western, *Calamity Jane*, and the comedy set in a factory, *The Pajama*

Game, she showed quite a lot of zest, and in her dramatic roles (such as *Julie*) she could even fly a passenger airliner without a minute's training.

Warners did not always rely on Doris Day. They also had on contract an even more insipid blonde, Virginia Mayo. Their men, like Fox's, were all more or less the same, bland and easygoing to the point of vacuity, even though their facial characteristics did make it just about possible to tell them apart. Gordon MacRae, for example, was pudgy while Dennis Morgan had a protruding jaw. There was also, of course, Ronald Reagan, whose most celebrated performance, without legs, in *King's Row* I had been too squeamish to see but whom I did watch in a profoundly forgettable item called *She's Working Her Way Through College* which, I suppose, encapsulated his Republican ethic.

Warner films, like Fox's, were worth seeing, if at all, for the lesser performers. In Fox films you could watch Charlotte Greenwood, at an advanced age, kicking up her legs like a contortionist, or Thelma Ritter, with a gravel voice that sounded like her name, insulting people right and left and being loved for it. Warners went in a good deal for winsomeness, principally by means of S. Z. Sakall, known sickeningly as Cuddles, whom Winnington told me to despise but for whom I could not help having a soft spot, since he reminded me of old men in synagogue who gave me sweets. Warners also possessed, as an antidote, the statutory friend to the heroine, Eve Arden who, like Thelma Ritter in the Fox films, was rude to everyone but, unlike Miss Ritter who really had a heart of gold, was rude for the sake of being rude and all the better for it. I prized the moment in *Tea for Two* – yet another formula film named after a decrepit song – where a minor character played by Billy de Wolfe, who was as usual portraying a cad, was struck by a woman he had wronged. Eve Arden, watching the scene with her usual sardonic glare, stepped forward with a look of utmost concern on her face but then, turning to the female aggressor, enquired anxiously, 'Did you hurt your hand?'

None of these moments, memorable to me if to no one else, had much to do with the films being musicals. Nor did I find I took to most of the musicals released by Universal studios, who specialized in hagiographic biographical works such as *The Benny Goodman Story* and *The Glen Miller Story*. It was during the latter that I conceived a firm dislike of James Stewart, whose excellent earlier films I was to see much later in revival, for trading pitilessly on

57

the hesitancy of speech for which most people liked him. In *The Glen Miller Story*, however, he more than met his match in June Allyson who, after an unspectacular career as a minor MGM star, was about to achieve public adulation in a series of roles in which she exploited her husky voice and shining nose to portray female long-suffering, this reaching its peak in a little number called *Interlude* in which she out-pouted Rossano Brazzi, no easy feat. It was only when, at a revival of *Words and Music*, I saw Miss Allyson brashly performing the Rodgers and Hart number 'Thou Swell', that I realized what a smashingly cheerful musical star she could have been if she had not found there was more money to be made by being put-upon and glum.

I had always had a soft spot for Paramount pictures. Recalling their 'Road' movies, I had great hopes of musicals starring Bing Crosby. Here again, though, I found that, unlike his appearances with Hope and Lamour, where things whizzed along, Crosby singing and not being funny was liable to hold up proceedings rather than advance them. Of course it was not his fault that Paramount decided to cash in on the success of the 'White Christmas' number in *Holiday Inn* by making a film based on the title of that song, nor was he responsible for the toe-curling scene in which tot ballerinas twirled around the screen. Nor indeed could he be blamed for the self-indulgence of one of his co-stars, Danny Kaye. Kaye had burst into pictures in 1944 in Samuel Goldwyn's *Up in Arms* in which, stationed in a cinema lobby, he sang a frenzied number guying the kind of films he was waiting to see. 'Manic Depressive Pictures Presents', he warned, 'Hello, Frisco, Goodbye'. Speedily and sadly, however, he surrendered himself to a deadly winsomeness. By 1952 in *Hans Christian Andersen* this reached a nauseating apotheosis in the lethal number 'Wonderful Wonderful Copenhargen' (that letter 'r' is not a misprint but an attempt to pin down the true awfulness of the way he pronounced the word), which did musically to the Danish capital what the frequently-filmed earthquake inflicted geologically on San Francisco.

Yet Paramount could make clever and unorthodox musicals too, the most witty being *Red Garters*, another Western, released in 1954, in which Rosemary Clooney, whose natural exuberance had been doused in *White Christmas*, exchanged insults with Guy Mitchell (an actor mainly noted previously for looking as if he had chronic mumps) against deliberately artificial sets in a small but charming confection directed by George Marshall. It was this same director who had created a new Hollywood personality for Marleen Dirty-tricks in *Destry Rides Again*. *Red Garters* contained lines which I regarded as the height of urbane wit: 'He broke the code of the West . . . He said a discouraging word.'

As I went to musical after musical, filled with hope each time that the revelation of *Singin' in the Rain* would at any rate in some small way be repeated, I was regularly disappointed. Not even *Singin' in the Rain*'s own studio MGM, could be relied upon. It too manufactured those awful biographies of faded songwriters (like Kalmar and Ruby, played in an incongruous partnership by Fred Astaire and Red Skelton, in *Three Little Words*). It too had on its contract list prim actresses like Kathryn Grayson and Jane Powell, kept on the books for their unrelenting soprano voices, and specialty performers such as Esther Williams, the aquatic giantess. In the early 1950s MGM inflicted on a deplorably willing public the chubby leer of Mario Lanza who, from *Toast of New Orleans* to *The Great Caruso* to *Because You're Mine*, got plumper and plumper until even his most adulating admirers would have no more of him and he was replaced physically (but not vocally) in *The Student Prince* by Edmund Purdom. Eventually, when the introduction of the wide screen provided sufficient space to accommodate the new and larger Lanza, he made a comeback, but it did not last. He died very young, too young to see his place as a fat tenor usurped by Luciano Pavarotti, whose only MGM musical, *Yes Giorgio*, had the distinction in the 1980s of being withdrawn before release, the equivalent of a book being remaindered before publication.

Seeing, new or revived, such MGM disasters as *Pagan Lovers*, *The Kissing Bandit* and *Two Weeks with Love* (starring the emphatically named Ricardo Montalban) I asked myself why it was that I was so disappointed with these pictures as well as most of the musicals made by other studios. When I thought carefully about them I realized that what they lacked, and what *Singin' in the Rain* contained in amplitude, was dancing. It turned out, to my surprise, that I was a dance addict. This realization greatly astonished me because I had always been bored to distraction by such ballet as I had seen on the stage, this appearing to consist of grown women wearing little girls' party frocks being spun around by men, often in wigs, whose underwear did not seem very efficient. Moreover, on considering the matter, what I found I

liked most was people dancing in groups. The corps de ballet in
Swan Lake at Covent Garden consisted of people doing approximately the same thing at roughly the same time. In *Singin' in the
Rain*, however, when the chorus in 'All I Do is Dream of You'
did their highly fetching little dance, they did absolutely the same
thing at precisely the same moment. They remained human but
became living patterns, and the effect was dazzling. Later on,
when I saw revivals of Busby Berkeley musicals, I was entranced
by his set pieces, in which battalions of girls became flowers or
musical instruments; however, these girls lost all identity (apart
from a fixed smile they had been ordered to assume) and they did
not really dance so much as move about as drilled units.

As well as discovering that, on the whole, it was the dance
musicals I really liked, I found that it was quite often not the
leading players who did the dancing I liked best. Hollywood
seemed to be populated with large numbers of people, men and
women, whom nobody had ever heard of and who hardly received
a mention in the credit titles, but who seemed to be able to
perform stunning acrobatic antics in strict time to the music and
absolutely simultaneously with each other: women like tall Ann
Miller, lively Marge Champion and perky Carol Haney; men like
the lithe Tommy Rall, the apparently ungainly (until he danced)
Bobby Van, and the preternaturally thin Bob Fosse.

Some of them would turn up in musicals produced by smaller
studios, of which the most exhilarating was Columbia's *My Sister
Eileen*, in which there were dance numbers (choreographed by
Fosse who soon gave up performing to choreograph, and later
took up directing) like 'Give Me a Band and My Baby' which
heaped invention upon invention until I hoped a way could be
found for it to go on for ever. Such performers were also to be
seen in little MGM films, which seemed to have been made almost
by chance or as some kind of afterthought, with titles like *I Love
Melvin*, *Give a Girl a Break* and *The Affairs of Dobie Gillis*.

I also discovered that some MGM producers, of whom the most
remarkable was Arthur Freed (co-author of the song 'Singin' in
the Rain'), had a strange kind of power over certain players who,
previously regarded as certain to blight any film in which they
appeared, came to unexpected life for possibly the only occasion
in their careers when galvanized by the material which Freed or
other producers provided for them. Thus, Esther Williams –
'Wet she's a star, dry she ain't', the droll Jewish comedienne

Fanny Brice had said of her – gave a witty performance opposite the always reliably sardonic Howard Keel, who portrayed Hannibal in a musical about ancient Rome called *Jupiter's Darling*. The doll-like Kathryn Grayson became a real woman, and a spitfire into the bargain, against Howard Keel once again, in *Kiss me Kate* which in addition contained an unbelievably complex number called 'From This Moment On' which was danced by Miller, Van, Fosse, Rall and, into the bargain, Carol Haney, later to become celebrated for performing the jerkily robotesque 'Steam Heat' in *The Pajama Game*.

It was indeed the sheer cheek – or daring – of MGM that took my fancy. They were not only prepared to make musicals set in ancient Rome but to adapt Roman episodes to more modern times, the Rape of the Sabine Women being the basis of *Seven Brides for Seven Brothers*. MGM's superiority was demonstrated when, in *The Second Greatest Sex*, Universal attempted a musical Western based on the *Lysistrata* theme which, despite the galvanic dancing of Tommy Rall, turned out to be a dud. *Seven Brides for Seven Brothers* was notable not only for some of the most inventive dance numbers ever seen on the screen ('Lonesome Polecat', set in the snow, and the barn-raising being especially spectacular) but also for turning the previously almost comatose Jane Powell into a spirited human being.

MGM could actually make baseball entertaining with, in *Take Me Out to the Ball Game* (re-titled *Everybody's Cheering* on this side of the Atlantic in order to entice the sensibly anti-baseball British into the cinemas), a comic number entitled 'O'Brien to Ryan to Goldberg'. They were willing to make musicals about serious, even solemn, topics such as post-war disillusion and in the course of doing so crammed *It's Always Fair Weather* (the last of the three films jointly directed by Gene Kelly and Stanley Donen) with numbers any one of which would have made a film miraculous. There was one sequence in which the three main dancers – Kelly, Michael Kidd (whom I had previously noticed only as a choreographer for *Seven Brides*) and Dan Dailey, up to then a gangling cipher in Fox musicals – danced on dustbin lids. There was another in which those same three dancers performed in separate locations but were edited into a unison trio through brilliant use of the split CinemaScope screen. There was yet another where Cyd Charisse danced with plug-ugly boxers in a training gymnasium, and another – 'Can It Be I Like Myself?' –

where Gene Kelly gyrated among traffic on roller-skates.

Even when MGM made back-stage musicals they were some-times not at all like other studios' back-stage musicals. *The Band Wagon* did, it is true, contain numbers performed on-stage and introduced by itemized programmes conned by an expectant audience: but these numbers did not take off into the clouds but strictly observed the unities of time and space. Fetchingly sung by Nanette Fabray, Fred Astaire and Jack Buchanan (whom I had previously written off as the grainy-voiced singer of a sloppy song called 'Goodnight Vienna', but who was here transformed into a performer of grace and wit) and directed by Vincent Minnelli, they were full of charm and humour. *The Band Wagon* also contained other songs performed off-stage to advance the plot. One, 'A Shine on My Shoes', danced by Fred Astaire in an amusement arcade, was filled with elaborate visual surprises. 'Dancing in the Dark' was suffused with a kind of nostalgic melancholy.

MGM could even make dream sequences tolerable. When she parted in rancour from her home studio Judy Garland, in a parody included in her self-pitying yet, to me, irresistible version of *A Star is Born* made for Warners, delivered the *coup de grâce* to all that mist and coloured lighting. MGM's *An American in Paris*, which was made three years earlier, included the mist and coloured lighting and just managed to get away with them, partly because the dancing was so superb, partly because the settings and characters in this long, climactic ballet were based on works by Lautrec, Dufy, Utrillo and other noted artists. These ingredients, of course, appealed to my continuing delusions of sophistication, as did the incident at the start of the film where Winston Churchill was depicted as a Paris pavement artist. Like most other members of the audience, sophisticated and otherwise, I was carried away by the Gershwin tunes and by the dancing of Gene Kelly, alone (plus winsome children) in 'I've Got Rhythm', with an old lady in 'By Strauss', and – in what was described as 'a sad rapt idyll' – by the river Seine with Leslie Caron in 'Love Is Here to Stay'. *An American in Paris* provided into the bargain my first prolonged exposure to the songs of George Gershwin.

An American in Paris was not always original. It pinched its method of introducing its heroine, through a series of split screen vignettes, from the 'Miss Turnstiles' sequence of *On the Town* (just as, I was later to discover, the 'Make 'Em Laugh' number from *Singin' in the Rain* was a crib from the 'Be a Clown' finale in Minnelli's *The Pirate*). It had rather more determinedly cute infants and stage Frenchmen than any film rightfully required. It was, however, very funny. Madge Blake, the gushing radio commentator from *Singin' in the Rain*, provided a cruel cameo of an effusive American woman buying perfume; Oscar Levant, through cinematic trickery, was enabled to perform as soloist and accompany himself in all the orchestral parts in Gershwin's piano concerto which, with smug self-satisfaction, he also conducted. It was agreeably and ostentatiously lavish (as in 'I'll Build a Stairway to Paradise', with a staircase which illuminated itself and statuesque girls posing as chandeliers) and astounding in its use of camera movement, particularly in the heart-stopping final crane shot that ended 'S'Wonderful'. After *Singin' in the Rain* it became my second favourite musical, and I pursued it wherever I could find it.

The revelation that musicals could be cinematic masterworks did not delude me into believing that *all* musicals must be cinematic masterworks. Most musicals that I saw turned out to be at best unimpressive, just as most other films I saw were unimpressive. Yet many, even the worst, had their moments of revelation and joy, and my discovery of them undoubtedly expanded my understanding of cinema. Much more important, the best musicals simply made my life happier than it would otherwise have been. Possibly I would have discovered them by myself at some time or other; but I knew then, and I know even more now, how much I owe to Speakman for dragging me along to see *Singin' in the Rain*.

LIGHTS, CAMERA, ACTION!

As I had travelled through my teens towards and into my twenties, I had come to know what I liked; but how was I to see more of what I liked? How was I to choose and how was I to judge? That was a question to which I returned repeatedly and to which I attempted in turn a variety of answers.

Of course, like most other picturegoers I had my favourite stars. Yet experience taught that although my favourites were always pleasant to watch, the films in which they appeared were not necessarily good just because they appeared in them. A movie with Veronica Lake or Abbott and Costello could be enjoyable or it could be painful; and which it would be was impossible to know in advance.

Of course, in addition, I selected films according to their subject-matter. I had started, as a child, liking comedies and adventure films and films with other children. In my adolescence I had gone on to enjoy detective stories and thrillers – though not horror pictures, anything with vampires and zombies filling me with dread – and some Westerns, and I had eventually come to have a taste for musicals. Yet some thrillers – *Phantom Lady*, or *Laura* – were successful (though the latter fell to pieces from the moment that the title character appeared, even though she was played by the haunting Gene Tierney) while others somehow were not. Generally I found that the ones that were not had sets that seemed made of cardboard and featured heroes who poked their guns round corners while tense music played, and then burst into rooms, opening cupboard after cupboard until without fail a body fell out of one. However, even thrillers with expensive settings did not always provide reliable entertainment. It was a puzzle.

Maybe a picture's place of origin had something to do with its quality. It was accepted truth in Leeds movie-going circles that British films were not much good and American films were a lot better though not perfect. Except for the Yiddish pictures shown at the Forum, no one living in Chapeltown seemed to know that films were made in any other country. Yet gradually, as the War had progressed, it became clear that some British films were turning out to be very good indeed, films like *The Lamp Still Burns*, about nurses, and *The Demi-Paradise*, about one of our noble Russian allies coming to Britain to give us the once-over. *Henry V* was memorable for me because I saw it on the same day in 1945 that my dog Peter began having the fits which caused him to disappear for weeks at a time and which eventually killed him. This film, which taught me that Shakespeare knew French and that they played tennis in his day, starred Laurence Olivier, as did the less instructive but more amusing *The Demi-Paradise*. There were also the films made by Michael Powell and Emeric Pressburger, including a most peculiar one called *A Canterbury Tale*, in which Eric Portman threw glue into girls' hair to prevent them going out with soldiers who, liberated from their distraction, were thus available to attend his wartime lantern-slide lectures.

Perhaps, then, the quality of movies depended on the studio that filmed them. As I entered my twenties I discovered that musicals made at MGM were generally better than musicals produced by other studios. Yet I also learned that musicals with the MGM label could be terrible; that although Twentieth Century-Fox manufactured dull musicals its thrillers were often exciting; that Paramount could make sharply funny comedies like *Nothing But the Truth* but also terrible comedies like *Monsieur Beaucaire*, and that both could star Bob Hope.

So, unless I went to absolutely everything – which I regrettably could not, lacking both the time and the money, though certainly possessing the inclination – how was I to choose? I began to notice something. *Five Graves to Cairo* had been a clever wartime thriller (with the letters spelling 'Egypt' on a map of North Africa concealing caches vital to the victory of the Allies) and *Double Indemnity* had been a compellingly sultry murder picture – and both had been directed by Billy Wilder. The credit titles of *Singin' in the Rain* told me that this picture was directed by Gene Kelly and Stanley Donen; and so, I was fascinated with my acumen for noticing, was *On the Town*, which I had also liked. *An American in Paris* was directed by Vincente Minnelli and so – surely it was more than coincidence – was another film I had much enjoyed, *Meet Me in St Louis*.

I had no real idea of what directors did in connection with their films, but I was certain they must be very important because their names were listed right at the end of the credit titles and all on their own, unlike Sidney Guilaroff and William Tuttle, the hair-stylist and make-up man for MGM, whose names were only part of a long list that there was not enough time to read. There was always time to read the director's name. Surely that must mean something? Of course, all those frames crammed with credit titles included the names not only of the hair-stylist and make-up artist but also the lighting cameraman, the editor, the composer of the incidental music, the author of the screenplay, the set designer, and all the others without whom a film of quality would not have been possible. I paid no attention to any of that. I got it into my head that how a film looked, how a film sounded and how a film moved were the sole responsibility of the director. Long before the intellectuals of *Cahiers du Cinéma* presumptuously presented the notion to the world as their own, all by myself and solely for myself I invented the *auteur* theory of cinema.

I began selecting the films I saw according to the name of their directors, and enjoyed happy hours of discovery as a result. For example, I found that Minnelli directed comedies and dramas as well as musicals, and that many of these were of high quality. Others, it had to be admitted, were not so good, but I loyally suppressed my misgivings about these. If I decided that I admired a director, it was my firm policy to find something worth praising in every film credited to him. Any other approach would, after all, have cast doubt on my initial judgement.

For example, it secretly struck me as ludicrous that in the melodrama *Undercurrent* the bedevilled heroine Katharine Hepburn – the victim of a frighteningly equivocal relationship with her menacing husband similar to that endured in *Suspicion* by Ingrid Bergman as wife to Cary Grant – was continually strumming on the piano bits of a concerto with only one tune, and that that tune was identical to the main theme of the third movement of Brahms' Third Symphony. Nevertheless I suppressed all doubts, even when in the film's finale a baby-faced Robert Mitchum turned this individualistic musical work into a piano duet.

As the years went by it became more and more difficult to enjoy Minnelli's work as the quality of his material deteriorated and his grip on it slackened, but I was still sitting there and hoping during a disaster like *The Sandpiper* (Richard Burton as a Clergyman

66

with Doubts) and the catastrophic updated remake of *The Four Horsemen of the Apocalypse*. Even at their worst Minnelli's films could always be relied upon to contain swooping camera movement, startling use of colour, imaginative use of extras, and one scene (known as his bizarre scene) which went right over the top, whether it was Lana Turner having extremely effective hysterics while driving a car (in *The Bad and the Beautiful*), or a boar hunt choreographed as if it were a ballet (*Home from the Hill*).

I offered every chance to Gene Kelly and Stanley Donen, both in tandem and separately. I gave up on Kelly first. He failed me not only with a painful comedy he directed, *The Happy Road*, which contained a tribe of children (who always brought out the worst in him) but also with the project which meant most to him. This was a musical called *Invitation to the Dance* which he created all by himself and which contained some mawkish broken-hearted clown sequences that made me want to break windows. I had a very low threshold of intolerance to mimes as well as to pantaloons: whenever Jean-Louis Barrault put on white-face in his revered role in *Les Enfants du Paradis* my reaction was one of irritation and impatience rather than the required empathic compassion.

Donen was more adaptable, and could even find some kind of residual quality in a deadly assignment like the film biography of Sigmund Romberg called *Deep in My Heart*. This was notable for a number featuring Gene Kelly dancing with his brother Fred, which demonstrated with agonizing clarity why Gene was a star and Fred was not. Donen could bring out the best in solid material such as the musicals *Seven Brides for Seven Brothers*, *The Pajama Game*, *Damn Yankees* and *Funny Face*, or the spoof thriller *Charade*. Faced with characterless, overblown comedies like *Indiscreet*, he showed that any individuality in his films reposed not in him but in the screenplays handed to him.

I had first picked out Nicholas Ray as a director whose work might suit me when in 1948 or thereabouts I saw *They Live by Night*, his thriller dealing with the travails of inarticulate young lovers caught in crime. Several years later Ray was confirmed in my regard by *Rebel without a Cause*, despite the bewilderment into which I was thrown by the opening minutes of this movie. When I read in advance about the high quality of *Rebel without a Cause*, I decided to prepare for it carefully by reading the book on which it was apparently based. I found a paperback edition, and settled down to study it.

It turned out to be about the hypnotherapy of a young psychopath, and much of its contents consisted of this disturbed person's induced memories of babyhood, even including his sensations when being wheeled along in a pram. I had not yet seen the film's star, James Dean, but had heard that he was a brilliant actor. I came to the conclusion that he would need to be during the scenes in which he was garbed in rompers and bib. It was a considerable surprise when I saw the picture and found that nothing whatever of the book had reached the screen apart from its title. I suffered an even more serious disappointment when, having enjoyed Dean's performance all the same, I sought out an earlier film of his which I had read about, *Has Anybody Seen My Gal?* Right at the start I was disturbed not to find Dean's name featured in the credit titles. I sat patiently through reel after reel and, after a while, was treated to a brief appearance – lasting, literally, no more than a few seconds – of Dean as a soda-jerk in a drug-store sequence. I waited for the rest of his performance, but after a very long wait indeed discovered that this did not exist; the drug-store scene contained his entire role, not really giving him the chance to build up a multi-faceted character.

Dean, of course, died tragically in a car crash after completing only three major pictures. Nicholas Ray, in a way even more tragically, went on to direct many more films. Struggling rather, I forced myself to admire (but had no difficulty in being fervently interested in) a ludicrous melodrama directed by him called *Johnny Guitar*, labelled the first Krafft-Ebing Western and notable for a gun duel between Joan Crawford and Mercedes McCambridge, the latter not all what she should be, the former everything she was expected to be. I lost patience with Ray in 1958 after dutifully attending a preposterous thriller he directed named *Party Girl*, though my tolerance had already been sorely tried by *Bigger than Life*. This latter dealt with the vicissitudes of a man suffering delusions as a side-effect of taking cortisone, the problem being that it was somewhat difficult to tell which were the cortisone delusions and which was the rest of the film.

I was always ready to go to a picture directed by Fritz Lang and, in the period when my friends and I were enhancing the revenues of Leeds City Transport, I had greatly relished the weird *Rancho Notorious*. This featured Marleen Dirty-tricks, still with a heart of gold, still ready to die for love, and still unable to pronounce the letter 'r', playing the queen of Chuck-a-Luck, the catchily-named bandits' hideaway. Lang went on to direct a sadistic thriller called *The Big Heat*, in which a pot of coffee was unfairly flung in the face of one of my favourites, Gloria Grahame, to whom I had given my heart when in *The Bad and the Beautiful* she kept saying, in a fetching Southern accent, 'James Lee, you have a very naughty mind.'

I was also at this time taken with another Lang production, a very sexy melodrama called *Clash by Night*. I did not know that this highly steamy film was adapted from a play by Clifford Odets, since I had never heard of Clifford Odets, but I did note that it was one of a large number of movies made at the time in which Marilyn Monroe wandered about in a minor role not seeming quite to know what to do. Lang also directed a swashbuckling pirate film called *Moonfleet*, adapted in a casual way from a novel by J. Meade Faulkner. In this George Sanders (not yet having failed to make his fortune in a project called Royal Victoria Sausages, for which he obtained and misused a British government grant, and for which misuse he was fittingly exposed by that scourage of anything connected with British royalty, William Hamilton MP) once again played a cad. Another star of the picture was Joan Greenwood who, having graduated from performing temptress roles in British pictures, arrived in Hollywood to portray still another woman no better than she ought to be though very aristocratic with it.

I consciously discovered George Stevens at the beginning of the 1950s, during a phase in the growth of my film appreciation which unfortunately matched a phase in his decline as a film director. I prided myself on being able to comprehend profundity. He was increasingly attempting to achieve profundity at the expense of his other undoubted talents. Stevens had been a very good workaday Hollywood craftsman who could turn his hand to any kind of film that was offered him, ranging from musicals to topical comedies. The best of these, *The More the Merrier*, dealing with overcrowding in wartime Washington, I had seen and enjoyed without realizing that Stevens had directed it, or even knowing that he was a director.

I came to know him by name when, in 1951, I saw *A Place in the Sun*. I was dragged along to this by Speakman who, having completed his Jean Simmons and Audrey Hepburn phases, had now entered an Elizabeth Taylor phase in, if anything, an even more heightened state of the calf-like adulation of which he seemed to possess inexhaustible supplies. With its swirling class conflicts, this polished melodrama perfectly suited my ponderously burgeoning political consciousness; and although Elizabeth Taylor at her most immaculately beautiful was indeed present, I was consumed with greater admiration for Shelley Winters, who had the double merit of playing the wronged working girl (with whom I naturally sympathized) and of still being slim.

So Stevens's next film came just when I was ready for it. Although the symbolism of *Shane* (including a villain dressed all in black) was pretty obvious even to me, it is fair to say that this was a very good Western indeed. It provided a fine role for Jean Arthur (whom I had seen as a child in *You Can't Take It with You*, which I assumed – wrongly – was funny because Mischa Auer did his comic Russian turn in it). *Shane* also contained a well-staged brawl. *Giant*, which followed, was a modern Western with an even bigger brawl, with Elizabeth Taylor – all efficiency among the Texan poor – even more beautiful and even more bossy over her menfolk, and Mercedes McCambridge repeating her butch role from *Johnny Guitar*. This time I was deceived by some fairly elementary inter-racial propaganda into believing that Stevens's latest film was something more than an extremely long soap opera. The anti-Nazi, pro-Jewish subject-matter of *The Diary of Anne Frank*, his next picture (with Shelley Winters again, by now getting pretty flabby), just about retained my loyalty to Stevens but in the 1960s, with the glutinous piety of *The Greatest Story Ever Told*, he finally lost me.

There were two directors, both of whom did have total control over their material, from whom I had to force myself to break away. I first encountered the work of the Frenchman Robert Bresson in about 1950 when Richard Winnington ordered me to to see *The Diary of a Country Priest*. I had no doubt at all that it was a marvellous film, with a performance by the young actor Claude Laydou which remains the most remarkable incarnation of human goodness that I have ever seen; but it was almost intolerably painful to watch as Laydou's priest died by inches before my eyes. After that I dutifully went to film after film made by Bresson and endured torments simultaneously with the suffering protagonists of his spare, merciless pictures. For me the limit came in the 1960s with *Au Hasard Balthazar*. It had been excruciating enough to watch humans being put through emotional and physical agonies, with the picture-making techniques employed by Bresson forcing me to watch every moment of their travails. This time, however, the Christ-like victim was a donkey, a donkey whose torments were depicted in huge close-ups of that beautiful, tormented head. I lived in continual terror of what Bresson's next film might make me go through, and then it suddenly occurred to me that there was no rule that said I was forced to see his pictures. Masterpieces as several of them were, they were not compulsory viewing, and it was perfectly legal for me to stay away from them. This, therefore, with a massive burden of guilt but also with an immense feeling of release, was what I proceeded to do. I felt deprived at missing further films of doubtless exceptional quality. I felt liberated from the burden of witnessing vast quantities of suffering.

In a similar manner I freed myself for some time from the brilliant cinematic inventions of the Indian director, Satyajit Ray. Dutifully, I had gone along to see his first film, *Pather Panchali*, made in 1954. I was in no doubt that I was experiencing an extraordinary screen début. I was equally in no doubt that I could not take much more of the same, harrowed as I was by the detailed depiction of poverty and deprivation and especially by the hauling off to her death of the family's 'auntie', whose verisimilitude was enhanced by the great age of the superb actress who performed the role. I stuck it out through the remaining two parts of this Apu (pronounced, for some reason, Upu) trilogy, and then, as far as Ray was concerned, decided to call it a day. Only a chance viewing much later of his comedy *The Chess Players* on television made me realize that it was possible to resume my acquaintance with this great director's work without flinching.

Luis Buñuel, on the other hand, outstayed his welcome with me less swiftly but more permanently. I had gone to his *Los Olvidados* at Leeds Tatler in 1950 and, while still watching it, was sure that I did not want to see anything more along the same peculiarly harrowing lines, which included the persecution of a legless person by sadistic manipulation of the crate on wheels which was his sole means of locomotion. All the same, in my earnest search for cinematic edification, I did subject myself to a revival of his early surrealist classic *Un Chien Andalou* and was puzzled into pretending that I had tumbled to its significance. *Un Chien Andalou* was, I pride myself, one of the very few films in which I allowed myself to become prey to the Emperor's New

Clothes approach to art. This lays down that if a work is pure rubbish and pretends to be a great deal more, informed cultural opinion is liable to join in fostering that pretence rather than tell the truth – namely that the work in question is pure rubbish. That work and the person or persons responsible for it then get away with an artistic fraud simply because of the fear of audiences and particularly critics of saying what they think about it, or even thinking what they really think about it. The principal film-maker who established a highly-lauded career as a beneficiary of the Emperor's New Clothes approach was Ingmar Bergman, who started out by making unpretentious if glum films. He then found out that, if he added to these confections such appurtenances as a skull or two, perhaps a gaping coffin, maybe people strangely garbed flailing each other in silhouette across the horizon, a clock with no hands or with hands speeding round its face, and other such empty, pretentious symbols, and if he added to that mixture several women of extraordinary beauty, he could persuade quite sensible people to acclaim him as a creator of genius rather than a self-important posturer.

I did not regard Buñuel as quite such a phoney or quite so dreary as that (for Bergman's films often seemed to me extremely tedious as well as portentously dour), but I did come to the conclusion that he was not all he was cracked up to be. I saw his *The Adventures of Robinson Crusoe*, thought it a humdrum little picture, and was then amazed to read essays on its limpid brilliance. Still, I went on giving him a try until I found that the horrible little trick in *Un Chien Andalou* of cutting an eyeball with a razor was repeated a quarter of a century later in *El*, in which a needle was pushed through a keyhole into an eavesdropper's eye, and yet again not long afterwards in *La Mort en ce Jardin*, with a prisoner sticking a pen into a jailer's eye. After this third example, I there and then pronounced for myself an interdict on Buñuel's work, and accordingly never did get to *Viridiana*, *The Discreet Charm of the Bourgeoisie*, or any of the other masterworks which, according to some of the most self-important critics in print, would have enriched my life. My life accordingly remains stubbornly impoverished. For a time I was shamefaced enough about my dereliction of duty to pretend that I had in fact seen some of these movies. I found that, by carefully reading the reviews in the quality press, I was able to discuss each of Buñuel's successive new works with at least as much authority as friends who had actually endured them.

There were some directors the basis for whose reputations among self-appointed cognoscenti completely escaped me. Samuel Fuller, acclaimed among cultists, seemed to me a manufacturer of works of extreme and reactionary brutality. Anthony Mann, admired in certain quarters for his Westerns, appeared unable to add to a film even the small curlicues of visual style that made it possible for a viewer to know that he was watching a film by, say, Carol Reed (whose visual preoccupation with staircases was always a source of interest to me). I acknowledged John Ford's technical competence, greatly enjoyed the sweep of Westerns he made in the ten years between *Stagecoach* (with, as embodied in Claire Trevor, the most attractive tart with a heart of gold in all cinema) and *She Wore a Yellow Ribbon*, and inevitably had been impressed by the social (if highly sentimental) realism of his film of the depression, *The Grapes of Wrath*. However, even in Ford pictures which I enjoyed, I always flinched when we got to the loutish comedy set-pieces in which John Wayne, Ward Bond and the other near-fascists who formed his stock company, punched, yelled, drank to the point of stupefaction and generally knocked each other around.

I began following movie directors in the same way that some of my friends followed football teams, and often with the same frustration, lack of discrimination, and unreasoning loyalty. During the years from my late teens onwards in which my cinematic knowledge (however superficial) and addiction (hopelessly incurable) grew in tandem, the output of a small batch of directors attracted me regularly to their films. Three of them worked in Hollywood, and the work of none of them justified use of the adjective 'great'. All, however, were supremely efficient and rarely if ever failed me. George Cukor did not write his own films, but chose, or was assigned to, movies which were extremely well scripted, often by Garson Kanin and Ruth Gordon. The movies of his best years (the late 1940s to early 1950s) lacked any discernible visual style – experiments with vivid and phantasmagorical colour came later, with such works as his strange and transfixing Western, *Heller in Pink Tights* – but were all noted for first-rate acting. I found that Cukor was skilled at eliciting effective portrayals from barely adequate performers, whom he could meld into an ensemble with such great players as Katharine Hepburn and Spencer Tracy (the father in a lovely little work called *The Actress*, in which Jean Simmons almost uniquely in her

73

Hollywood career was perfectly cast as a young girl in a provincial community who insisted against her parents' wishes on going on the stage). Tracy and Hepburn made many films together and became a screen institution as a movie team, but it was almost solely in Cukor's films (Stevens's *Woman of the Year* being a spritely exception) that they were provided with material which matched the high standard of their talents. *Desk Set*, an office comedy, was clumsy, and *Guess Who's Coming to Dinner*, racially patronizing and sickeningly sentimental, won a reputation by fraud simply because Tracy made it while he was dying.

John Huston and Billy Wilder were both writers as well as directors. Wilder began in the early 1940s with sparkling comedies. I particularly liked *The Major and the Minor*, in which Ginger Rogers posed as a 12-year-old child in order to travel on a train at a reduced fare and was found out by my beloved Diana Lynn. The pseudo-child's love affair with Ray Milland seemed innocent at the time, although twenty years later it would have been banned as sexually perverted and twenty years after that would have explicitly depicted a consummated affair with a real child. Wilder next proceeded to make a series of *films noirs*, which became ever more extravagant and which, always impressed by the lurid rather than the understated, I thought tremendous. In the humiliating scene in *Sunset Boulevard* in which Gloria Swanson takes her fledgling gigolo, played by William Holden, out on a shopping expedition, I was much impressed by the insinuating remark to Holden by the sales clerk: 'As long as the lady's paying for it, why not take the vicuna?' – even though I had not the faintest idea what a vicuna was.

The first film of Huston's that I saw knowing it to be his was *The Asphalt Jungle*, one of a number of robbery films – which later, when mixed with comedy, came to be known as 'capers' – in which the crime is successful but the criminals are not permitted to keep their loot. Kubrick's *The Killing* and *Rififi* (the thriller which rehabilitated Jules Dassin after his victimization in the Hollywood witch-hunt), together with many others, were to follow. Huston's own *The Treasure of the Sierra Madre* was constructed on the same principle; there is, after all, only a limited range of basic story plots, and the charm of such films lay in the exposition rather than the storyline.

I had become an admirer of Huston, without having seen an inch of celluloid exposed under his direction, after reading *Picture*, by Lillian Ross. This indignant volume claimed that butchery by MGM executives had mutilated a potential masterpiece, *The Red Badge of Courage*. I was completely persuaded that evil had been perpetrated, and developed an especial loathing of the movie's producer, a harmless, indeed well-meaning, man named Gottfried Reinhardt (son of Max). I eventually tracked down *The Red Badge of Courage* to the Ritz, Leeds, where it was playing as a second feature, and found it to be an unexceptional piece of work. Its unimpressive qualities may quite likely have been due to the incompetence of Huston's original concept but, as far as I was concerned, poor Reinhardt was indubitably the culprit. As I watched Huston's further work I noted that, apart from whatever responsibility he might have for the screenplay, his contribution to the film was limited to setting up the shots and supervising the actors, and that when the material was no good he could do nothing to cure it. In the 1980s his screen version of *Annie* was to achieve distinction as one of the most incompetent, because so badly scripted and edited, musicals ever made; yet *Wise Blood* and *Fat City*, made during roughly the same period, were magnificent because their ingredients were magnificent.

Immediately after the war, Italian cinema did the screen world a disservice by introducing the concept of neo-realism, and so launching the practice of labelling films according to arbitrary stylistic genre. New Wave and cinema vérité were to follow, their vocabulary, like that of neo-realism, being absorbed into every commercial film that followed. Fellini, who came along later in the day and battened on what others pioneered, struck me as an Italian Bergman, but cruder. Rossellini emerged as a director who had in the aftermath of the war made the most of material that could not fail (like *Rome*, *Open City* and *Paisa*) but turned into a posturer when he tried to ascend beyond inspired film journalism into empty symbolic melodrama like *Stromboli*. Luchino Visconti may claim to have started the neo-realism movement with *Ossessione*, his wartime version of *The Postman Always Rings Twice*, which he followed with *La Terra Trema*, an impressive pseudo-documentary about poverty among Sicilian fishermen. However, he soon moved on, with the dazzling *Senso*, to his true métier of visually dazzling, highly operatic melodramas.

Having read that Visconti was indignant at the way in which his Hollywood distribution company had shortened, re-edited and ruined the colour quality of the English-language version of *The*

Leopard, I precipitately flew to Paris, where the full print was on view at a small cinema off the Champs Elysées. I received an extra reward when, prowling round the Louvre, I came upon the original of the Greuze painting featured in one of Burt Lancaster's most heavily significant scenes. I bought a postcard of this and kept it as a memento inside the sleeve of the soundtrack recording of *The Leopard*, which thus became a double souvenir resting on the shelf next to a record of Bruckner's Seventh Symphony, also featured in this highly cultural movie. Several of Visconti's pictures – including *Death in Venice* as well as *The Leopard* – were visually so ravishing as to vanquish all attempts at balanced criticism; some, like *The Damned*, set in Nazi Germany, were so overblown as to be absurd; and all of them, from his earliest neo-realistic works onward, were absorbed in prolonged contemplation of beautiful young men.

Vittoro de Sica was far more consistent, and I followed him faithfully through four successive works of genius – *Bicycle Thieves*, *Shoeshine*, *Miracle in Milan* and *Umberto D* – all of them dealing with poverty and privation, three of them ending hopelessly, and one (*Miracle in Milan*) choosing the joy of fantasy rather than the misery of reality for its conclusion. The performance of Emma Gramatica as a doting foster-mother who turns into an angel depicted the one old person who was allowed to be happy in the entire corpus of de Sica's neo-realistic work. De Sica made an essential contribution to these marvellous films, but he was no more an *auteur* than any of the other directors I came to admire. His genius was an ability to transfer almost flawlessly to the screen the scripts of Cesare Zavattini. Once the pair of them got into the grip of Hollywood, as personified by David O. Selznick, the realism, neo or otherwise, was squeezed out of their films by commercialism and the star system, and their great collaborative work came to an end.

Although I allowed enthusiasm, of which I possessed much, to overwhelm judgement, of which my stocks were limited and easily exhaustible, I did come to realize that just as no star and no studio could guarantee quality, so not even the name at the end of the credit titles of even the most fashionable, talented or dedicated director could of itself ensure a pleasurable or uplifting evening. I did, to my credit, eventually learn that one film-maker stood out above all others, and that a picture was most likely to approach perfection if it was directed by Jean Renoir. Of course, Renoir too was dependent on collaborators. Nearly forty years after I first saw it, in my adolescence, the very title *Une Partie de Campagne* could bring instantly to my mind not only this tender film's languorous summer images but also the seven notes which provide the melting theme of the music composed by Joseph Kosma. The camerawork for this film and for *La Grande Illusion* was provided by Renoir's nephew, Claude, who also worked on his uncle's wistful film set in India, *The River*. He did not, however, photograph *La Règle du Jeu*, which many regard as Renoir's masterpiece but which I could not like completely because of the slaughter of birds during the shooting scene. For me *La Grande Illusion* remains Renoir's masterpiece, a film about war which, unlike others with a deservedly high reputation such as *All Quiet on the Western Front*, does not simply say that war is wicked but goes on to exalt humanity above war.

La Grande Illusion became for me one of the two greatest films I had ever seen. The other was *Battleship Potemkin*. In my league tables (and I used to compile many, including lists of favourite politicians, for I did have interests apart from the cinema) Eisenstein vied with Renoir for top place among directors. Squeamishly, I could not bring myself to see *Strike* (because of its scenes in an abbatoir). I did see *Potemkin*, and its sequence on the Odessa Steppes – which, like the Grand Canyon and Persepolis, is one of the very few renowned phenomena which outstrip their advance publicity – left me goggling. *October*, or *Ten Days That Shook the World* had, in sequence after sequence, such as that of the flashing wheels of the bicycle brigade, caused me to realize that film editing possessed dazzling possibilities. I had, however, also seen *Ivan the Terrible* which, although assured of its magnificence, I thought stagey and static. So I did not know what to make of Eisenstein; and that was good, because I was beginning to realize that in cinema there could not be an acknowledged top ten whose merits were universally accepted.

As I went to film after film, gazing and goggling at what was presented to me, I realized that I was going to have to make up my own mind. What was more, my opinion was as valid as that of anyone else. As I set out on a voyage of exploration I realized, to my terror and delight, that I was on my own.

6

FLASHBACK

At the age of eighteen I had travelled to Oxford to compete for an exhibition. The short time I spent in that city upset me profoundly. I fell in love with it instantly, but was sure that I had no chance whatever of gaining entry to its university. There was a series of examinations, followed by a *viva voce* test. At this latter form of interrogation I spent a good deal of time attacking Laurence Olivier's film of *Hamlet* which was then currently on release and which, like so much of that generally over-rated performer's work, had been absurdly lauded. I have to admit that my opinions on the inherent hilarity of Ophelia's death scene, with that much put-upon lady floating down a stream smothered in petals, were plagiarized from Winnington's cruel but accurate review in the *News Chronicle*. I am not sure whether I had even seen the film at the time. However, these views were almost certainly the only apparently original ideas I expressed on paper or in person during this short but intense period of scrutiny.

I returned to Leeds deeply depressed at what I considered a brief and cruelly finite taste of life at Oxford. Arriving home from school one day not long afterwards, I found almost hysterical excitement. A telegram had arrived with the news that I had won the exhibition.

At Oxford most aspects of university life (apart from work) preoccupied me happily. I celebrated my election as secretary of the Labour Club by inviting Richard Winnington, in a way responsible for my being in the place, to speak at a tea meeting. He accepted, and his name was printed on the club programme, attracting requests for permission to attend not only from non-members of the club but from non-members of the university as well. I was not alone in my enslavement to this autocrat. Tragically, the week before he was due to come he telephoned to say that he would have to cancel; Peter Lorre was bringing a new film to London and the private view conflicted with his engagement at

Oxford. Anyhow, I had actually spoken to my instructor, and was stirred by the glamour of his reason for not coming.

Oxford was, of course, very close to London. However, although friends kept going there, it never occurred to me to go too. I had hardly been to London in my life, and the place seemed to belong to an almost unattainable world into which it would be foolish, perhaps even dangerous, to trespass without some convincing reason. So during my four years at Oxford my only visit to London was as part of a coach party to help Dr Edith Summerskill retain her marginal seat at Fulham in the 1950 election.

Anyhow, why should I go to London? The city of Oxford itself contained sufficient cinemas almost to slake my appetite and, if that grew excessively voracious, there were picture houses round about with names (if I recall accurately) such as the Regent, Kidlington, which could be visited with minimal trouble. Oxford itself contained the usual first-run cinemas owned by the major chains, at which I kept up my basic film-going. It was also enriched by two repertory cinemas, and at these I began to fill in the gaps that the full but somewhat stodgy diet of Leeds movie-going had failed to satisfy.

After trailing through the rain-washed streets up beyond Worcester College to the Scala, or enduring the travails of Oxford's eccentric bus service out to Headington, I would sit open-mouthed watching old glories that were new to me. At last I saw Greta Garbo and, witnessing her torments photographed with that curious MGM lighting that made everything look as if it had been filmed in silver, understood why everyone at home had talked about her as if she was some kind of goddess. I had never seen an actress who did such delicate things (as in the scene in *Queen Christina* which I later learned was famous but which I thought I had picked out for myself, in which she memorizes all the objects in a room by touching them) or who spoke in a manner that seemed to caress the words as they left her lips. Although I found the anti-Communism in *Ninotchka* crude and even repulsive – going as I was, through a very left-wing phase at the time – I was on the side of the Russian lady commissar all along, and eventually realized that this was not only due to Garbo but also to Ernst Lubitsch, this being my first experience of his work.

When I was really quite a small child, I had heard elder members of my family talking in puzzled tones about a film called *Citizen Kane* which seemed to have been made in an incomprehensible manner; a brother-in-law of mine had left it after ten minutes, completely mystified. My only experience of Orson Welles as a director had been *The Lady from Shanghai* but, that having been before my *auteur* phase, I had thought of the film as a very good thriller starring the luscious Rita Hayworth and with an extraordinary climax involving the shattering of a hall of distorting mirrors. I realized that someone very clever must have thought up that stunning effect, but I had not at the time bothered finding out who. Of course I had seen Welles in *The Third Man* and had much admired his speech about the Swiss inventing the 'coo-coo' clock, being greatly taken with this apparently idiosyncratic pronunciation which, I assumed, was peculiar to him rather than, as I learned much later, being common to all citizens of the United States.

Of course I had come to know that *Citizen Kane* was regarded as something very special indeed, which was why I hurried along to the Scala when it was revived there. I was extremely disappointed. If I had seen it when it had first been issued, in 1940, and had I had the intelligence at that time to understand the nature of what I was being shown, I would undoubtedly have been staggered. When I saw it for a second time, some years later, I had accumulated sufficient knowledge of what had preceded it in cinema, and had gained sufficient insight into the nature of scripting, set construction, camera placement and editing, to be overwhelmed by Welles's achievement. Then and there, in Oxford, I was able to compare it with *The Bad and the Beautiful*, which I had just seen at the Super cinema, and which had borrowed both Welles's style and his methods to create a delightful if unimportant entertainment. Accordingly, *Citizen Kane* came as a let-down to me and for some time afterwards I thought and spoke of it disparagingly.

On the other hand, my introduction to W. C. Fields and my reacquaintance with the Marx Brothers were altogether more satisfactory. Fields I knew little if anything about, not even having seen him as Micawber in *David Copperfield*. I was utterly enchanted by his bulbous nose and his nasal, sing-song voice. I could not make very much of *Million Dollar Legs* (I had assumed, before seeing the film, that the expensive limbs of the title belonged to pretty girls rather than competitors in the 1932 Olympic Games) which was not surprising, since I learned that this film, like others starring this prodigy, had been made in conditions of extreme chaos. However, I instantly took the view that this shameless, incompetent, highly put-upon person was one of the great men of the twentieth century, an opinion consolidated by others of his works and totally confirmed by the moment (in *It's a Gift*) in which he attempted to murder a noisy tradesman, seeking to lure him to his doom with the wheedling summons: 'Oh, vegetable man!'

Fields was a loser, especially against children. Groucho Marx, to whom Winnington had introduced me but most of whose work I met in Oxford for the first time, was a winner, against everyone with the foolhardiness to encounter him. I saw all the then available Marx Brothers films, from *Animal Crackers* through to *The Big Store*, and, thinking things through, decided that the Brothers as a group left me cold. Chico's obligatory piano solo bored me out of my mind, as did Harpo's turn on his chosen instrument; and I was not much further enthused by Harpo's dumb antics with motor horn and other equipment. Watching the MGM comedies, which came after their earlier and more manic Paramount works, I was further irritated by the banal plot episodes that linked the comedy scenes and the vacuous supporting players who sang songs.

It was, though, the set pieces in Marx Brothers films which first reduced me to uncontrollable heaving sobs: the cabin scene in *A Night at the Opera*, the *Travatore* climax from that same film, the piece-by-piece demolition of the train in *Go West*, and the eerie finale of *At the Circus*, with an orchestra playing Wagner floating away, as any orchestra playing Wagner should, across the water and into infinity.

Yet the more I saw of the Marx Brothers, the more I realized that the one I came to see – indeed, the one I would have quite liked to be – was Groucho. I was enchanted by the way he walked and the way he leered, I adored his grating singing voice, as in his rendering of a ballad called 'Lydia the Tattooed Lady'. Above all, however, I was impressed to the point of distraction by some of the things he said, most of all by the scene in a saloon in *Go West* where, having lost consciousness and being in process of having some water administered to his lips, he suddenly jerked to life and, thrusting the water away, demanded: 'Brandy! Force brandy down my throat!' When I became active in politics Groucho Marx, far more than Aneurin Bevan or Demosthenes, was to have, for better or worse, a fundamental influence over my speaking style.

I also became re-acquainted with Chaplin. I had previously known him chiefly as a man in a bowler hat and with a Hitler moustache (having seen *The Great Dictator* at too early an age I even thought for a time that Chaplin and Hitler were the same person) and who pranced around with a walking stick in a jerky way – his silent films being projected, without my knowing it, at the wrong speed – and who thoroughly failed to amuse me. When I saw *City Lights* I realized through my tears that the man was a very great artist indeed. However, I avoided testing this judgement to destruction by deciding to avoid *Limelight* altogether, descriptions alone of its subject matter sufficiently nauseating me.

When my days of cinema-going and occasional study at Oxford came to an end, I returned to base at Leeds and began applying for jobs. This process of disappointment and humiliation lasted for several months. From time to time it required visits to London, the expenses for such journeys being paid by prospective employers. These included one Norman Kark, the proprietor of a short-lived glossy magazine called *Courier*, who, from a dispiriting office above Trafalgar Square, wearily but decisively rejected me despite a reference from a prominent back-bench Labour MP, Denis Healey, whom I had unaccountably impressed during an Oxford Union debate in which he as a visiting speaker had joined me in opposing the establishment of the Commn Market. On another humiliating occasion I was dismissed – kindly but firmly – by a journalist clergyman, who did not regard me as suitable for even an unimportant vacancy on his upmarket comic periodical for children, *Eagle*. I always solaced myself for such failures with a visit to a West End cinema before returning home in dejected disgrace. Accordingly, I was well ahead of my gainfully employed friends in Leeds in seeing such works as Mankiewicz's (and Shakespeare's) *Julius Caesar*, a curious production filmed on the left-over sets from *Quo Vadis* (which I had not seen) and interpolating the battle of Philippi filmed as a B picture Western into some magnificent speaking of Shakespeare's verse.

Eventually one of these interviews resulted in the offer of a job, Assistant General Secretary of the Fabian Society. In some ways this post, which I took up at the beginning of 1954, suited me very well. Leading Labour politicians like Harold Wilson, Richard Crossman and Anthony Crosland were members of the Fabian executive committee, and I had quite a lot to do with them. Executive meetings often took place in committee rooms in the basement of the House of Commons, and accordingly I visited frequently a building with which only the MGM studios in Culver City could compete for my devotion. The job itself was not really much of anything, combining under an august title a number of dogsbody duties. I did not mind that at all. What I would have preferred was more money. The gross – if such an adjective was not inappropriate – pay amounted to less than £9 a week. While I dutifully bought my *Manchester Guardian* – then, as later, the noticeboard of the Labour movement – every day, on Sundays I sometimes had to choose between a newspaper and lunch. All I could afford for my living accommodation was a minute bed-sitting room in Stamford Hill, in East London, and much of my income was consumed by the fares (653 trolley followed by 76 bus) to distant Westminster.

In a sense, though, these straitened circumstances were actually an incentive to cinema-going. I did not particularly wish to spend much time in my bed-sitter, particularly since at that time I could not afford a radio for indoor entertainment (the days of cheap transistors not yet having arrived). Nor could I manage regular holidays. So I would get out to the cinema as often as I could afford the cheapest seats, and instead of going away at holiday times I would use my allotted four vacation weeks for spells of concentrated cinema-going. It was not often that I was able to go to picture houses in the West End though, when they knew I longed to see a particular new film as soon as possible, girlfriends would loyally share the cost of admission.

However, there was no shortage of cheap picture houses in London at that time. Not only were there numerous chain cinemas belonging to Rank and ABC, including two advantageously situated in Stamford Hill itself. All over the place could be found little halls, some of them owned by the Classic chain, others entirely independent, showing films going right back to the beginning of sound. These places lured me with the glitter of an Ali Baba's cave stocked with celluloid and, thanks to them, I began in a random but comprehensive way to learn the technical and historical vocabulary of the sound cinema. I came, too, to realize that directors and stars with whose work I was familiar had not sprung into existence simultaneously with the growth of my interest in films, but had pasts that were both fascinating and revealing.

Even more required as regular reading than the *Manchester*

Guardian was *What's On In London*. This ill-written but essential publication provided details of food at restaurants I could not afford and theatres whose presentations did not interest me very much, live entertainment being in my opinion a scorned runner-up to the treasures of the silver screen. To me, the only section of *What's On* worth reading was that which listed, in alphabetical order, all the films on show on weekdays throughout London; the Sunday movies were not similarly tabulated, and had to be found in a further search of programmes printed cinema by cinema in minute and sight-destroying type. Combining a study of *What's On* with the tube and bus maps, I toured London from corner to corner in search of cinematic enlightenment. I came to know Ealing and Islington, Hampstead (with its indispensable Everyman) and Baker Street (which housed the best of the Classics, and where I remember seeing, awe-stricken, an understandably eager Woodrow Wyatt almost jumping the queue in his fear that he would miss the start of *Ziegfeld Follies*). The Ionic, Golders Green, attracted me no less than the Granada, Tooting. It was at the Granada, Tooting, that I savoured a rarity, *New Faces*, which first displayed Eartha Kitt to the world. If a film-going test had been instituted similar to the 'Knowledge' to which taxi-drivers are subjected, I would have passed *summa cum laude*.

So I saw legendary – but to me, arcane – Hustons like *The Maltese Falcon* and *Key Largo*. Both of these sent me to revivals of films starring Humphrey Bogart and, belatedly but gratifyingly, I sat shivering with pleasure through a masterpiece hitherto unknown to me, *The Big Sleep*, in which I at last made the acquaintance of glamorous Lauren Bacall, née Betty Perske. *Key Largo* engendered an admiration for Edward G. Robinson who, in turn, opened for me the delights of the funniest gangster film ever made, *A Slight Case of Murder*.

I acquainted myself with Hitchcock's English period, from the innovations of *Blackmail* to the melodramatics of *Rebecca*. The latter scared me until explanations started, when like *Laura*, another film with an absent title character, it seemed to me to disintegrate. I saw the legendary *The Philadelphia Story*, one of the most immaculate of George Cukor's comedies, and was at last able to understand how Katharine Hepburn had managed almost by force to compel audiences to admire her.

I saw films directed by Robert Wise (long before he became flabby and sloppy in hugely expensive and characterless musicals like *The Sound of Music* and *West Side Story*) and especially relished his harsh, spare boxing film *The Set Up*, so much truer than the lauded *Champion*, and containing the repellent fight sequence with the blind man urging on: 'Go for his eyes! Go for his eyes!' Max Ophuls had already moved into his bloated period, during which for a time he knew brief commercial success with the modish and sexy *La Ronde* and *Le Plaisir*. I went to his much more affecting *Letter from an Unknown Woman*, in which Joan Fontaine gave her most touching performance as a vulnerable woman betrayed into love, and was exhilarated by the obsessively perpetual camera movement that led James Mason, who had worked with Ophuls in *Caught*, to pen a poetic salutation that rhymed 'Max' with 'tracks'.

Up to that point I had only seen the later comedies written and directed by Preston Sturges. Now I caught up with the earlier ones: *The Great McGinty*, a brutal but very funny political film; *The Palm Beach Story*, which astonished me by showing that Claudette Colbert's range went far beyond the coy and sentimental to which I thought she was limited; and, above all, *Sullivan's Travels*, which was to have such an effect on my cinematic taste that it changed my outlook fundamentally. Having enjoyed Colbert in one stunningly witty film, I at last saw her in *It Happened One Night*, the first movie in which I found the smirking Clark Gable tolerable, and one which astounded me by demonstrating that the range of its director, Frank Capra, went far beyond the folksy and nudgingly endearing, which I had previously regarded as his inescapable characteristics.

Ninotchka had introduced me to the work of Lubitsch. I now travelled backward in time with him, as with other directors, and found that with *The Love Parade* and *Trouble in Paradise* he had been involved in musicals that had pioneered cinematic innovations such as dialogue in rhyming couplets. Through these films I learned, too, that Maurice Chevalier, of whom I had thought, if at all, as a Nazi collaborator with a repellent chuckle in his voice, was a performer with wit and style, and that Jeanette MacDonald could be more than a horse who sang soprano.

As I plied my way around London, a cinematic Flying Dutchman happily doomed never to rest in any geographical area or cinematic period, above all I caught up with the past of the movie musical. I saw *Forty-Second Street* and learned that musicals could be both adult and dramatic, as well as hard-boiled in their humour. *Forty-Second Street* revealed to me the kaleidoscopic hallucinations of Busby Berkley. These I pursued through all their charm and vulgarity in films containing sequences which demeaned women as few others ever have, reducing them to items in a complex design but creating bewitching patterns in the process.

The small part played by Ginger Rogers in *Forty-Second Street* (as well as in the non-musical but almost flawless tragi-comedy *Stage Door*) caused me to trace that lady's career and at last to see the musicals she made as partner to Fred Astaire. Unlike the later MGM musicals on which I doted, they were not seamlessly constructed. They seemed to consist of conventional comedy peopled by agreeably droll stock characters, interspersed with musical episodes which were often not production numbers elaborately and lavishly staged, but duets between the two principal dancers, of whom Astaire was clearly the dominant partner.

Sadly, I could never recapture the peculiar pleasure that my sisters had experienced as they saw these films one after the other during a short five-year period in the 'thirties. Then, as picture followed picture, enjoyment accumulated and was enhanced through the opportunity to watch the relationship of these two gradually develop on screen; what they had been to each other in *Top Hat* provided a kind of sub-text to what they did with each other in *Carefree*. Although I recognized that Astaire was far more brilliant than Gene Kelly, I never came to like him as much as Kelly, partly because, in his most astonishing gyrations, he seemed to be saying 'Look at the extraordinary things I'm doing', whereas Kelly just got on with it. Yet as far as I was concerned, even when Kelly was performing with a supreme fellow-artist like Judy Garland, he never achieved the effect of a comfortable and developing relationship that shone like an aura round everything that Astaire and Rogers did together. These two did not simply dance as a couple; they danced as one.

At last, too, I filled in the gap that existed for me in Judy Garland's career between *Meet Me in St Louis* and the inflated but transfixing weepie *A Star Is Born*. It was not until much later that I was able to hunt down her celebrated final great number for MGM, 'Get Happy' in *Summer Stock* (a film which, when I saw it, seemed to me even more notable for the intricate and melancholy 'You Wonderful You' which Gene Kelly performed with a newspaper and a creaking floorboard as partners). During this period of force-fed education I did, however, at last catch up with the other three sequences which demonstrated to me that no woman in musicals could hope to compare with Garland: 'Be a Clown', with Kelly in Minnelli's *The Pirate*; 'We're a Couple of Swells', with Astaire, in *Easter Parade*; and, above all, *The Harvey Girls*, a musical about pioneering waitresses in the American West. Although for most of its length *The Harvey Girls* was almost repulsive, it contained the most exhilarating sequence I have ever seen in any musical film, 'On the Atchison, Topeka, and the Santa Fe'. This hugely complex piece of organization – shot, I was to learn later, in a single take – featured many dozens of performers, but despite the intricate mechanics that interwove camera and dancers, with Garland at the centre it seemed as simple and natural as the pure pleasure it exuded.

During these few years I used to go to the cinema most days, sometimes every day. There were days when I went twice, even three times, though I did find that three times a day verged on the indigestible and four times (which I tried) was simply too much. The cinema had by now become a sweet obsession with me, into which everything else had to fit. In 1955 I stood for Parliament in the, for Labour, hopeless seat of Bromley. Even then I interrupted my election campaign to go up to central London to see Minnelli's *Brigadoon*; and a good thing too, for it ran for only a short time and I would not readily have missed its 'bizarre' sequence, a night-club scene in New York whose sound-track was overlaid with memories from the intolerably quaint Scottish village of the title. *Brigadoon* was a village which, under a curse, came back to life for one day every century.

Sitting in the dark in often dingy auditoria, watching films made long ago, I was imprisoned in my own time warp; but far from being cursed, I was a happy prisoner who would have been appalled if threatened with release.

7

VOICE-OVER

———

I had never wanted to be an engine driver. Nor, to the disappointment, possibly even grief, of my parents, had I so much as considered becoming a doctor, a dentist or a lawyer. From the moment I discovered politics, during the 1945 election, in a corner of my heart lay the hope of becoming a Member of Parliament, a hope I rarely articulated because I regarded it as beyond possibility. In any case, I had to earn a living, and the calling which most attracted me was journalism. The form of journalism to which I especially aspired was film criticism. Richard Winnington died in 1953, and like Katharine Hepburn in the solemn George Cukor film of that title (in which the co-star, Spencer Tracy, did actually portray a writer) I thought I could be 'Keeper of the Flame'.

After my brief period at the Fabian Society I managed to obtain employment on a newspaper, but not at first as a writer. Instead, in 1954, I was recruited by the *Daily Mirror* as research assistant to the Labour MP Richard Crossman, who was at the time writing for that newspaper, then at the height of its political influence, a twice-weekly column of comment. Even columns of comment must contain a fact or two, and these facts should ideally be accurate. Dick Crossman, for whom I quickly developed a deep affection combined with a readiness to murder him, did not see facts in that way. To him they were an obligatory but regrettable decoration on the perfectly cooked soufflé of his opinions, and he could be highly casual with them. However, under Hugh Cudlipp, its editorial director, the *Mirror* had an obsession with factual accuracy which became deeply engrained within me. How could it not, when I would be required to spend a whole afternoon checking whether there was a hyphen between the Lloyd and the George in the name of the then Home Secretary? So I was torn between Crossman's romantic approach and Cudlipp's wish for absolute precision (I being on Cudlipp's side) and reconciling their requirements became a full-time (sometimes over-time) job which I greatly enjoyed but which at the same time maddened me.

So I was prepared for a leavening of this demanding diet; *Forward* came along to provide it. I had intermittently read this non-conformist socialist periodical, which was published in Scotland but distributed in a random and ineffectual fashion here and there in the rest of Britain. Now I heard that it was to move its office to London, theoretically to spread the message of the Labour Party throughout our islands, but in fact to counter from the right the influence of the weekly *Tribune*, at that time edited by Robert Edwards, later himself to become a senior Mirror Group journalist. Edwards had been a serious disappointment to me since, when sharing with him a Tribune Brains Trust platform in a small town called Baldock, in Hertfordshire, I gave him the serious advice that *Tribune* was in need of a film critic and that I filled the bill to perfection. Edwards tried me out for a few weeks and, despite an especially perceptive review of *Carmen Jones* which he consented to publish as a contribution to the campaign against racialism, he most shortsightedly decided not to continue with my services. Accordingly, while my political views remained considerably closer to those of the *Tribune* of the 1950s (which in the 1980s would have been regarded as soft left), I was all in favour of *Forward* as a platform for a cinematic alternative to the scrawlings of whoever Edwards was at the time employing to review films.

Accordingly, I made it known that I was, as it happened, opportunely free to take on the responsibilities of movie criticism for this new venture. The new editor of *Forward* was Francis Williams, former editor of the *Daily Herald* and for a time press secretary to Clement Attlee during that gnomic figure's premiership. I went to see him in his minute and disorderly office in High Holborn, only a short step away from the *Mirror* building, Geraldine House, itself no less disorderly though of larger dimensions. Coughing a good deal over a cigar, and thus proving himself a thoroughgoing journalist in this respect if in no other, Williams questioned me closely as to my approach which, with deep cunning, I endeavoured to tailor to whatever approach his somewhat disjointed remarks seemed to indicate that he himself had in mind. He told me that he wanted not simply political criticism but relevant criticism, whatever that might be, and I hastened to assure him that it was this very kind of criticism and no other that

I myself aspired to write. Without further ado I was taken on. I suppose that some kind of fee was offered and accepted, quite certainly of a highly exiguous nature, since Williams, with the exception of himself and his deputy John Harris (later to be Lord Harris, a member of a future Labour Government and a defector from the Labour Party to the Social Democrats not long after that), was not in the market for staff journalists but sought his writers among workers for other publications moonlighting from their full-time employers.

More important than any trifle that Williams agreed to pay me was a small expense allowance. I would, of course, have taken on the job for nothing, and indeed quite possibly would have been ready to make a small payment myself in return for doing it; but since my activities for *Forward* turned out to involve me in considerable financial outlay, it was as well that I received recompense for that. For my life as a part-time film critic was hectic to a degree. Each day I would go into the *Mirror* offices and carry out my duties in the meticulous manner that Cudlipp expected and Crossman relied on. Often, I might work late, sometimes very late indeed. During the morning, the fallow time of the working day for any journalist employed by a daily paper, I would telephone film distributors and cinema managements to organize my complimentary admission to the latest films. I was determined if at all possible not to miss a single new movie, however insignificant; for I was mindful that small classics like *The Window*, *Phantom Lady* and *They Live by Night* had been buried by bashful or unenlightened distributors and resuscitated by vigilant critics.

Because of my duties at the *Mirror* I was unable to attend the day-time press shows to which regulation critics were invited. Instead I went to advance previews which some distributors organized, and which were held in the evening; or, where this was not possible, I saw public performances, a procedure which required liaison by telephone with incredulous cinema managers. Most of these had never heard of *Forward*, and quite understandably did not see why they should surrender – to someone whose obscure bona fides they had to take on trust – tickets for which more plainly sane patrons might pay with ready cash. Nevertheless, almost invariably I was granted admission. I then had to plan my evening.

I could not leave the office until I had completed whatever assignment I had been given. Once released, I would tear away and run for the nearest appropriate bus or tube. At that time there were so many new films that I often had to see two in an evening. This meant a careful study of timings if I was to fit them in and, if possible, eat a meal between showings. Elegant restaurants were excluded both for reasons of time and financial exiguousness, and I became a habitué of Golden Eggs and pancake houses. Previews arranged by major companies were most satisfactory, since some generous distributors provided refreshments as an implicit bribe to reviewers. I always liked going to the Twentieth Century-Fox private theatre in Soho Square, which offered a sandwich or two in an ante-room prior to showing, in a viewing room so luxurious as to be almost sinful, a film which would, unfortunately, rarely measure up to the quality of the service, this being a time when the Fox product was not at its most distinguished. Still, if I was to see the almost ludicrously shapely Jayne Mansfield in *The Girl Can't Help It* or the almost entirely fleshless Suzy Parker in *Kiss Them for Me*, this was the place to do it.

I also became a satisfied occupant of the most expensive seats in the most sybaritic West End theatres, the Carlton, the Plaza, the Empire, the Leicester Square Odeon, the Warner and the Curzon. There was one evening of marvels almost too rich to digest when, after seeing Minnelli's superb new comedy *Designing Woman* (Gregory Peck, Lauren Bacall, Dolores Gray) at the Empire I hastened, with no time even for a sandwich, straight across Leicester Square to the Odeon to see the best of Donen's solo musicals, *Funny Face* (Fred Astaire, Audrey Hepburn, Kay Thompson). By the 1980s it was almost impossible to see two films of such quality in a year; I was able to exult in both of them in the space of less than five hours.

I went, also, to the fringe first-run cinemas now mostly vanished: the Odeon, Tottenham Court Road, where Universal-International would smuggle into the fringes of the West End the pictures it was least proud of, and the Berkeley, at the southern end of the same street, a cinema of almost blatant seediness, which specialized in showing solemn Soviet films but whose real attraction – insofar as it possessed any at all – was that it was conveniently situated near to a Lyons Corner House (now also gone) where I could eat flapjack drowned in cream or some beans on toast before proceeding to my next celluloid treat. This might be a Finnish anti-war tract or a Brazilian thriller, a nudist documentary (in which persons of unprepossessing physique, just about discernibly differing in sex, would be observed from a determinedly decorous standpoint primly playing volley-ball, apparently the only activity that nudists ever indulged in if cinematic records were to be relied upon as evidence) or an Australian saga depicting the virtues of workers' solidarity.

Determined to judge each on its merits, however unobvious these might at first appear, I saw them all and wrote about them all. *Forward*, to be fair, never failed to publish what I wrote, or at any rate a portion of it. At the *Mirror* I had watched sub-editors at their tasks, men like a modest, hesitant sort of fellow whom we called Larry Lamb, after the self-effacing little animal in the 'Toytown' stories, and who was later to gain a knighthood and lose his hesitancy, not to mention his modesty, as editor of the *Sun* and then of the *Daily Express*. I had grown to admire the finesse with which they cut a story to fit it to the space available (which was carefully sketched out on a plan of the page). These were the skilled surgeons of journalism. *Forward*'s sub-editor – at any rate the one responsible for dealing with my copy – was a butcher, and a bloody one at that. Not for him the delicate carving up or out of a paragraph. Instead he simply stopped my article short at the point where the room for it was exhausted, even if this meant cutting it off in the middle of a review or even the middle of a sentence.

This was certainly one method of sub-editing and, in its way, indubitably effective. Having laboured lovingly over my prose, I was ready to take a carving knife to whoever was responsible, if only I could trace his identity. I was later told that the sub-editor was in fact someone whom I came to know well and indeed to like. His name was Roy Roebuck, and a few years later he was to sit briefly as a Labour Member of Parliament for a previously safe Conservative seat, won almost by accident in Harold Wilson's 1966 landslide. During his period in the House of Commons Roebuck endeavoured to organize a group in support of Wilson when the going for the government got rough, and named this band of zealots the Young Eagles. To me the mayhem he committed on my copy for *Forward* made him seem, rather, a Young Vulture or even a Young Carrion Crow. Whether or not it was 'relevant' in the manner Francis Williams had ordained, I was proud of what I wrote and wanted it to be read in the state in which it emerged from my dedicated labours.

It really did seem to me to be pretty good. I looked for merit wherever I might find it, however unlikely the film. I spared a good word for, of all things, a British rock musical, *Don't Knock the Rock*, on the grounds that it was at any rate lively; and even I discerned a moment of genuine terror, which I dutifully commended, in *The Monster That Challenged the World*, a film about a huge man-eating snail. I looked for new artists whom I could claim to discover and indeed found some. One was the comedy actress Elvi Hale ('The British screen's most delightful comedy discovery since Kay Kendall', I called her), whom I erroneously singled out for future stardom. Another was the director Stanley Kubrick whom, on the basis of two early thrillers, *Killer's Kiss* and *The Killing*, I accurately prophesied to be 'one of the cinema's brightest future prospects'.

I looked for small, unpretentious films (such as the British adventure story *Campbell's Kingdom*) to which I could, in so far as anyone read a word I wrote, provide a boost. I took a particular pleasure in deflating what I regarded as pretentiousness. *Twelve Angry Men*, a film much admired at the time (and even more so later) for its depiction of one man's fight for justice – with the one man played by Henry Fonda, Mr Integrity himself – received short shrift. I denounced it as 'a phoney social tract, wallowing in self-conscious righteousness'. Employing an adjective which I clearly found useful, I denounced another film that received even more solemn adulation, *The Bridge on the River Kwai*, as being 'as phoney as they come'. 'All we get is a mass of slushy philosophizing,' I railed. I rebuked the director, John Ford, by that stage of his career almost deified, for 'over-sentimentality, juvenile slapstick, and a tendency to let things get out of control'.

My determination to demonstrate to *Forward* readers that no detail, however minute, escaped my eagle eye, was ostentatiously to the fore: 'The film record of some of the Moscow Bolshoi Ballet's performances in London last year was shot, we are pompously told, in Dr Paul Czinner's "Special method and technique". The equipment for this method and technique included, apparently, one camera with a grubby lens and another that was out of focus.'

I really had it in for certain performers. Casting a cold eye over a remake of *The Hunchback of Notre Dame*, I alleged: 'A plea of temporary insanity would be the only possible excuse for Anthony Quinn's drooling performance as hunchback Quasimodo.' Dispassionately examining Otto Preminger's *St Joan* I said of Jean

Seberg, later to become a cult figure in Jean-Luc Godard's *Breathless*: 'Her death at the stake should be a tragic sight. To the audience it comes as a welcome relief.' Poor old Cathleen Nesbitt, doing her game best at an advanced age in a sickening piece of work called *An Affair to Remember*, was denounced for giving 'an indescribably hateful performance'.

My greatest savagery, however, was reserved for Deborah Kerr. Reviewing Minnelli's *Tea and Sympathy*, I offered the baneful warning that this highly-regarded star 'seems in grave danger of becoming a second Greer Garson. Her performance is an embarrassing collection of facial contortions, vocal distortions and fluttering gestures.' Even these remarks, however, were generous compared with my account of her activities in *Beloved Infidel*, the appalling film about Scott Fitzgerald's love affair with the Hollywood columnist Sheilah Graham. 'Her performance,' I reported, 'is something of a triumph. For it is accomplished almost entirely with the hands. When Miss Kerr wishes to convey sadness she presses one hand against her eyes. For horror, a hand is held to the stomach. Hands outstretched, held to mouth and wrung together, in that order, signify various phases of worry and bewilderment. And a swift downward movement from forehead to nose, to mouth, to hips, followed by a dart back to the neck, means that Miss Kerr is undergoing a transport of misery.'

Clearly, I fancied myself as a humorist, not to say a satirist. Sometimes I sought to be funny in an affectionate manner, as in a description of the plot of *The Gypsy and the Gentleman*, a bizarre confection directed by the intellectually inclined Joseph Losey which I recommended to all collectors of bad films: 'Ingredients include a hidden will, an heiress imprisoned in a folly, a madhouse, whips, gambling, half-castes, drunkenness, nudity, bastards, seduction, slapping, a lady marrying beneath her station and a scandal talked of throughout the county.'

My most scathing assault, of which I was extremely proud when I wrote it, and which could not have been more heavy-handed if I had tried, was reserved for a Fox weepie. '*The Gift of Love* tells the story of Julie (Lauren Bacall), Bill (Robert Stack) and Hitty (Evelyn Rudie). Julie and Bill, even after five years of marriage, Love Each Other Helplessly. Bill is an Absent-Minded Genius who needs Looking After Like a Baby. Julie learns she is Dying Of An Incurable Disease. So she adopts little orphan Hitty to look after Bill, When She is Gone. She teaches her how to help him on with his clothes, pour his coffee, and put a rose on his breakfast tray. But Bill hates Hitty. He sends her back to the orphanage as soon as he gets back from Julie's funeral. One night he has a Supernatural Experience which leads him to rescue Hitty, who has fallen over a cliff during a whimsy mood. Julie then appears to them both in a Vision From Beyond The Grave. The film ends with Genius and Orphan landed with each other for life and Julie well out of it all, which could account for the smirk on her face as the trick photography fades her off the screen.'

So I proceeded on my way, having a whale of a time and not really doing any harm to anyone but myself, on whom I was inflicting serious eye strain and a dangerously unbalanced diet. Then one day I received a telephone call from Charles Wintour, editor of the London *Evening Standard*. Would I come and see him in his office in Shoe Lane? Intrigued by the invitation, I sneaked out of the *Mirror* building and kept my assignation. It turned out that Mr Wintour actually read *Forward*. Moreover, his reading had spread to my film criticism. He had noted my review of William Wyler's re-make of *Ben-Hur*, a movie of massive prestige which had received rave notices from all critics. All except one, that is. My indictment of this massively expensive epic was severe: 'Director William Wyler, with his squad of five script-writers, has decided on a glutinously reverent approach. This provides us with a ghastly little prologue full of heavenly choirs and pious sentiments, long stretches of utter boredom, a genteel orgy, astonishing bouts of sadism, and an attitude to the story of Christ that (for example, in its assumption that the sole purpose of the crucifixion was to cure Ben-Hur's relatives of leprosy and so provide the film with a happy ending) must surely repel Christians and nauseate unbelievers.' Not content with this tirade, I even denounced the film for its technical shortcomings: 'Too obvious use of models and surprisingly incompetent matte work.'

Wintour had noted this outburst and been, in some fashion, impressed by it. He was looking for a new film critic and among others he told me, he was considering me. Here I was, actually with a prospect of fulfilling my life's ambition and becoming a full-time film critic for a highly regarded (if conservatively-inclined) newspaper. The dream did not, however, last very long. Wintour was soon in touch to let me know that he had chosen someone else, Alexander Walker in fact, who was to become one of the longest-serving of all Fleet Street movie-reviewers. Vain about my writing, I could not understand why I had been rejected. Much later, Wintour told me that he did not think I would have been happy working for a Tory paper. Little did he know that, if it had meant earning my living by going to the pictures every day, I would have been ready to consider an offer from *Der Stürmer*.

Disheartened but ever game, I went on with my pieces for *Forward*, still the victim of Young Eagle-to-be Roebuck's blood-stained cleaver, finding virtue wherever I could (as with 'Loyal Grigg's perfect photography in crisp VistaVision Technicolor' for the obscure Western *The Jayhawkers!*), still puncturing what I regarded as pretentious, as I declaimed – in my review of Margot Fonteyn's film *The Royal Ballet* – against 'ensemble dancing so ragged that no director of a Hollywood musical would tolerate it'. I even attracted attention from a film-maker. I said of the Tommy Steele musical *Tommy the Toreador* that 'it was a drab effort featuring the pleasant, if meagrely talented, Tommy Steele', and that 'its best moments achieve the level of those depressing B pictures turned out by Hollywood in the mid-1940s'. Writing from Elstree Studios, the film director, John Paddy Carstairs, paid a tribute: 'Your Mr Kaufman's review was delicious. I'll frame it and have it on my desk on the set.'

This belated attention was encouraging in its way but, sadly, the game was up. *Forward* ran out of money and ceased publication, and I had to go back to a normal existence in which I went to the cinema less frequently and paid for my ticket when I did go. So life proceeded for four years, during which I toiled on at the *Mirror*, adding to my duties as a researcher occasional and then more frequent assignments as a political writer. I was getting on in my trade, even if my trade was no longer catering to my cinematic obsession. Then, in 1964, I received an approach from the *Listener*. This journal, at that time principally a collection of transcripts from BBC broadcasts, but with a books and arts section of high repute, was edited by Maurice Ashley, a historian with a deservedly considerable reputation whom I did not know and had never met. However, I did know the *Listener*'s deputy editor, Oleg Kerensky, grandson of the Menshevik Russian Prime Minister and a contemporary of mine in the Labour Club at Oxford. He had in fact served on the solemn tribunal which I, as chairman of the club, had been required to set up to inquire into the alleged misdeeds of an Australian undergraduate at Worcester College.

This student, an Australian called K. R. Murdoch, was an engaging, if somewhat buccaneering, character. He decided to stand for office in the Labour Club, and challenged a hard-working student by the name of Jones for the post of secretary. There was at that time a rule that prohibited canvassing in the club's elections. Few candidates openly disregarded this rule, though a certain amount of covert and discreet electioneering did take place; as much, in the characteristic British way, as could be got away with. K. R. Murdoch decided to blast his way through these effete Pommie evasions. Far from furtively, indeed almost blatantly, he ran an energetic campaign. Others were also active on his behalf. Such a challenge to convention could not be disregarded. Formal complaints were made to me as chairman, and under the rules I was required to set up a tribunal to investigate the alleged offences.

This awesome body consisted of all ex-chairmen of the club still in residence, an eminent collection of persons who included not only Kerensky but also a popular woman undergraduate named Shirley Catlin. 'The Bloody *Tribb*yanal', as the irreverent K. R. Murdoch immediately dubbed it, approached its duties with great solemnity, hearing witnesses and taking evidence. The whole proceeding lasted quite a time, and its outcome was awaited in the hopeful anticipation that it would be thoroughly scandalous.

The coven of ex-chairmen discovered that – whether with or without K. R. Murdoch's knowledge was never entirely clear – what would later have been called a campaign team had either been formed or formed itself. One zealous activist was an unusual Eastern European, possibly a Yugoslav, a certain Dr Boris Roniger, whose role at the university – if indeed he was actually a member of it – had never been precisely established but who was to be encountered at any meeting or other event even remotely connected with left-wing politics. Another was named McIntosh.

The Bloody *Tribb*yanal deliberated, and found that K. R. Murdoch and his supporters had indeed contravened the anti-electioneering rules. It then delivered its verdict. Murdoch and McIntosh were banned from candidature in future elections, but since Dr Boris Roniger had never been a candidate for anything and might not have been eligible to offer himself even if he had wished to do so, no very firm action against him was thought desirable or even, perhaps, possible. He went on attending every conceivable meeting, as before.

McIntosh lived down his youthful indiscretion, was elected to the Greater London Council, became leader of its Labour Group, and was subsequently appointed to the House of Lords: proof, if any was ever needed, that crime does not pay. Murdoch returned to Australia on hearing of his father's sudden death and began to work his way up in the family business, which was newspapers. This was the first stage of Rupert Murdoch's downward path to millionairedom and control of most of the world's communication media. Shirley Catlin married a man named Williams and, so far as I can gather, carved out some sort of career for herself in politics.

Kerensky, apart from finding employemnt with the *Listener*, wanted to be a theatre critic almost, though not quite, as much – for no other's aspiration could hope to equal mine in intensity and ardour – as I yearned to be a film critic. I had put him in touch with *Forward*, and they had obligingly taken him on, he adopting for that purpose, for reasons no clearer to me now than they were then, the nom-de-plume of Anthony London. The *Listener* was looking for a film reviewer, and Kerensky had suggested my name to Maurice Ashley. To my delight, Ashley decided to give me a chance, once again on a freelance basis.

This time, however, the pace was much more leisurely: no scurrying from cinema to cinema, no pancake houses or Wimpy Bars. The *Listener* looked not for a weekly bulletin but for a monthly essay. They did not require coverage of all new films but, instead, a disquisition upon movies of my choice. I was free to see as many films as I wanted in order to make my selection, and that meant that I was once again able to attend previews. This change of pace called for a change of style. The terse journalism which, with gratitude, I had learned at the best school of journalism in Britain, the *Daily Mirror* editorial floor, was to be replaced with longer sentences and more sententious (possibly pretentious) judgements. I still aimed to seek out the unusual and to puncture the over-rated, but I did so in a way which I hoped would provide diverting reading for the readers of an intellectual weekly. Not at that stage having read his work, I did not realize that I was trying to rival the feat of the greatest of all American film critics, James Agee, who had written simultaneously for *Time* magazine and the *Nation*, the American counterpart of the *New Statesman*.

In *Forward* I had briefly described films in the British 'Carry On' series as 'admirably unpretentious' and 'very funny'. For

Listener readers I attempted a more profound analysis: '*Carry on Cowboy* is not so much a film as a succession of animated picture postcards of the kind at which censorious watch committees are apt to purse their lips. Here they all are – the bosoms (handy as holsters for pearl-handled revolvers), the bottoms (ready, as required, for kicking or pinching), the lavatory jokes (a gratuitous chamber-pot sets the trend in an opening sequence) and the really quite gross phallic symbolism. To the refined *cinéaste*, seated in the chaste semi-isolation of a "specialist" cinema, such goings-on might appear at best naive, at worst vulgar, and, either way, dimly unfunny. But in a crowded circuit cinema – its audience filled with popcorn, salted peanuts, fruit juice sundaes on a stick, and an entire readiness to sit and be entertained – *Carry on Cowboy* is bound, and rightly, to attain success in its simple objective of arousing laughter without any ancillary requirement of deep cerebration.'

To my new – I trusted – captive audience in the *Listener* I paraded my favourites, such as a more mature Audrey Hepburn, whom I praised (in Donen's comedy-thriller *Charade*) not only for her 'finely-honed comic timing' but also for 'the wistful swoop of the swan's neck on the fledgling sparrow's body'. I even lauded films with Elvis Presley. I was, beady-eyed, on the look-out for exponents of that arch-crime, phoneyness and, right at the start of his career, singled out the cinematic fussiness for the sake of fussiness that was to impoverish Francis Ford Coppola when he had achieved eminence enough to own his personal studio. 'In *You're a Big Boy Now* chapter heads are in evidence. So are interspersed, out-of-time episodes, as in *Ulysses*. So are typed sub-titles, as in *The Group*. So is film projected in negative. So is wild track. So is stop-motion.'

I was, indeed, extremely keen to demonstrate my deep (in truth, limited and rudimentary) understanding of the technicalities of the medium, saying of the musical *How to Succeed in Business without Really Trying* that its 'basic material has so much verve that some of it survives even the De Luxe Color photography, apparently carried out in a crypt with the aid of sodium lighting'.

Unknown to me, my exhibitionistic erudition did serve a valuable purpose. It was the policy of the *Listener* to enrol its film essayist for a year at a time. When the allotted twelve months ended, so did the reviewer's stint. This had been made clear to me at the outset; I knew that all I was getting was one year's treat, and was perfectly content with that. As my period of tenure drew to an end, Ashley began looking for a replacement and decided upon the extraordinarily distinguished writer J. R. Ackerley, himself a former editor of the paper. However Ackerley, when approached, declined Ashley's offer. He asserted that he could not possibly maintain the level of knowledge that he insisted, with embarrassing flattery, displayed itself in my work. Ashley asked me to continue. I was staggered that someone who wrote as beautifully as Ackerley should in any way regard me as his superior, but I accepted like a shot, and continued, on and off, until 1967.

During this time my principal occupation, the one that earned my salary, changed twice. In the autumn of 1964 I left the *Mirror* to become political correspondent of the *New Statesman*. The *NS* was then a journal whose editorial policy, extraordinary as it may appear in restrospect, sought to attract readers by elegant writing and an attractive lay-out. Its later brutalistic policy of poor paper, ugly typeface, screaming headlines, columns of statistics replacing text wherever possible, and (where printing it was unavoidable) text which was deliberately unreadable – and ungrammatical too – had not yet been defiantly and suicidally adopted. John Freeman, the editor who recruited me, had no objection whatever to my continuing my film writing; so throughout my year at Great Turnstile, working from a cupboard round the corner of the stairs, I wrote for the journal that was employing me and at the same time for one of its principal competitors. The world of the weekly reviews being what it was, no one saw anything odd about this arrangement.

Then, from the *New Statesman*, I went to work as parliamentary press liaison officer at No. 10 Downing Street, this title concealing or at any rate obfuscating my role as Harold Wilson's political press adviser. I asked Wilson if I could continue with my *Listener* reviews, and he made no objection. This was scarcely surprising, since Wilson, as President of the Board of Trade twenty years before, had done much to foster the British film industry, and he continued to take an interest in the movies. This did not, however, mean that he went to the cinema much himself. At No. 10 Downing Street his principal pastime was being Prime Minister, which he regarded as a spare-time hobby as well as a full-time job. However, with the assistance of his personal secretary, Marcia Williams, herself a film addict though not quite on my scale, I did manage to lure Wilson to the pictures a couple of times. On each occasion the cinema had to be warned in advance, since it would not have done for the Prime Minister to turn up and find that there was no room for him or have to queue. In any case, accommodation needed to be found not only for him but for his two Special Branch bodyguards who accompanied him everywhere, though to what purpose was not entirely clear. When I asked one of them what he would do if someone shot the Prime Minister he replied, without a moment's hesitation: 'File a full report.'

If Wilson did wish to go to the cinema, even the title of the potential film had to be vetted. A visit to *Fiddler on the Roof*, for example, would simply not be possible, leading as it inevitably must to ribald jokes in the press and jeering cartoons into the bargain. *Till Death Us Do Part*, which was seen at the Columbia cinema in Shaftesbury Avenue, was regarded as ideal. It stemmed from a popular television series and it contained a bigoted Tory (Alf Garnett) who met with suitable humiliations throughout. It also suited the Prime Minister who, despite the massive sophistication and subtlety of his approach to politics, had simple tastes when it came to artistic matters, liking nothing better, for example, than to sing interminably lengthy extracts from the libretti of various intolerable works by Gilbert and Sullivan. Travelling by train to his Merseyside constituency he would join in duets with his wife Mary, he tunelessly, she with impressive musicianship. Their repertoire included not only light opera, but hymns as well. The need for him and his party, on security grounds, to travel secluded in a reserved compartment, deprived fellow-passengers from gaining an enlightening insight into their Prime Minister's personality.

Wilson knew by heart a great many of the works of Shakespeare, too. On one occasion he made a trip to the Round House in Chalk Farm to see a more than usually gloomy production of *Hamlet*. When he visited the actors backstage at the end of the performance, he seemed somewhat to discomfit Nicol Williamson, who played the title role, by easily outquoting him from the play's text. Wilson was so impressed by this outing that he recommended the Round House *Hamlet* to various American statesmen, including one president; though all of them, possibly having a taste for something more cheerful, failed to accept the Prime Minister's advice and go to see it.

The other film to which I accompanied Wilson was *Hello Dolly!*

– yet another directorial failure by Gene Kelly – at the Odeon, Marble Arch. Otherwise, he left me to go on my own, the understanding being that in doing so I would not neglect the work I did for him. I was indeed conscientious about my Downing Street duties; but the hours were exceptionally long and it was inevitable that I would eventually stray. My misdemeanour occurred when I received an invitation to a press show to be held at the London Casino, then a kind of entertainment hermaphrodite, never quite sure whether it was a theatre or a cinema. Its auditorium later had administered to it a kind of sex-change operation which turned it into an undoubted theatre, by name the Prince Edward, which was chosen as the receptacle for a gruesome but, inexplicably, immensely successful, pseudo-musical named *Evita*. The film in question was *2001* and since, despite my disappointment with its predecessor, *Dr Strangelove*, I remained a fanatical admirer of Stanley Kubrick, I was determined to see this new production, even though the showing was to take place during the morning, when I should have been at work. I therefore sneaked away up Whitehall and into the alleys behind the National Gallery that led to Old Compton Street.

Unfortunately for me, I was seen in the picture-house by a junior minister (though what he was doing there, when he should have been governing the country in accordance with his appointment, was not entirely clear) who, in complete innocence, mentioned my attendance to someone else. This inevitably got back to the Prime Minister, who one way or another heard everything, and led to a good deal of roguish finger-wagging from him. This episode might indeed have been the source of his conviction that I could never be relied upon to follow any project through, a complaint he would voice to me on every conceivable occasion, even when I was patently following something through at that very moment. Despite this lapse, no attempt was made to inhibit my cinema-going or film-reviewing, and indeed the latter came to an end not through any edict from the Prime Minister's study but because at last the *Listener* did find a replacement for me, however inadequate, and my term of service was belatedly brought to an end.

It was a shame in a way, since I had enjoyed it greatly. However, pressure of work at No. 10 was making both the attendance and the writing more and more onerous, and I could not have kept it up for very much longer. After my stint with the

Listener, I was occasionally commissioned to write about films for other publications. A magazine called *Town* had the ambition of providing brief film recommendations in a section at the beginning of each issue, rather on the lines of the listings in the *New Yorker*, and asked me to write them. However, neither the assignment nor, indeed, *Town* itself, lasted very long. The BBC radio arts programme *Kaleidoscope* from time to time invited me to review films, some of them very odd indeed. I was glad to accept, but found such assignments no challenge, since this undemanding labour required me to write nothing but simply to go to the film and be interviewed about it.

The magazine *Opera* greatly flattered me by asking me to review Joseph Losey's film of *Don Giovanni*, thus launching me on a sporadic career of opera-reviewing for other publications (and enabling me to see the only film by Losey that I ever wholly enjoyed) but not really providing me with any genuine prospect of earning a living by writing about the very few operatic films that were made. In essays for the *Listener*, to which I returned as a regular writer in the 1980s, I was at liberty to refer to movies whenever I wished, which may have been somewhat more often than my readers found strictly tolerable; and I contrived to get hold of film books by writing periodic reviews of these for the same publication. However, I had eventually to resign myself to the realization that I was never going to become a full-time film critic and that I would have to make do with the fulfilment of my alternative ambition of becoming a Member of Parliament.

8

LOCATION SEQUENCE

———

Although my addiction to the cinema had developed to the point of becoming an overpowering craving, it had never slipped over the bounds of reality into fantasy. In the standard manner, I had from time to time, as intended, identified with this hero or (less acceptably) with that villain; but I had never shared the itch of my Leeds friend Wood actually to become part of the on-screen action. Nor, indeed, had it occurred to me for a moment that I might appear in films as an actor.

True, during my long-ago Leeds Grammar School days I had taken part in the ventures of the school dramatic society, graduating from playing a highly realistic First Witch in Macbeth, via Nurse in *Romeo and Juliet*, to the plum role of Sneer in Sheridan's *The Critic*. I achieved a massive success as Nurse, principally because I transformed it into a broad comedy role, with the line 'Ay, ay, the cords', as the show-stopper of the evening. Not only was this not what Shakespeare intended, it was not what the producer (an enthusiastic master reduced to chronic despair by his performers' taking control of the play) instructed. Indeed, at one performance the laughter of the audience – highly relieved that all those lines of blank verse were unexpectedly being turned into entertainment – during the scene intended movingly to depict the discovery of Juliet's body became so great that the curtain was hastily rung down. In the brief unscheduled interval that followed, my remaining lines were removed from the script. After this, Sneer came as an anti-climax, since all I could think up to enliven this languid character's part was to keep falling off my chair, an approach to the role which did not entirely match the sophistication of Sheridan's social comedy. I indulged in these antics because I did not really enjoy acting, which appealed to me even less than driving a fire-engine as a possible calling in life.

Nor, especially having noted the torment inflicted on our schoolmaster producers by young actors, did I in later life have the tiniest inclination to direct older performers. Again, appalling clumsiness – due, I always held, to the curse of left-handedness – prevented me from even being able to wind a watch, so the idea of learning how to work anything so complicated as a movie camera, or to patch bits of films together, never occurred to me. Accordingly, a career either as a cameraman or an editor was out. Writing was different. I felt I knew how to put words together, but I did not envisage those words being spoken by actors. I wanted them to appear in print and to be admired for their style and pungency by newspaper readers.

There did, however, eventually come a time when I began to write scripts. In the autumn of 1962, by now an employee of the *Daily Mirror*, I was visiting Leeds for the weekend and was watching television in my parents' flat on Saturday night. There appeared on the screen the first edition of a new programme, claiming to be satirical, by the name of *That Was The Week That Was*. I watched its topical sketches with interest and, what is more, with a certain degree of annoyance. I was certain I could do better.

What I needed was an idea and, having none of my own immediately to hand, I borrowed someone else's. The *Mirror* group's editorial director at this time was Hugh (actually Hubert, but he concealed this significant item of information even from *Who's Who*) Cudlipp. Cudlipp, a short (and short-tempered) Welshman, was a newspaperman of genius. Under his control the *Daily Mirror* became for a time Britain's – and probably the world's – greatest and most influential mass-circulation newspaper. Some of the people he employed were hacks, for example Jack Nener, editor of the *Mirror* when I joined the paper, who once in my hearing offered the authoritative definition: 'A fairy is a man who gets out of the bath to piss.' They were always, however, skilled hacks, for Cudlipp both required and respected expertise. Having been for a while minded to sack me as surplus to requirements, he gave me a reprieve upon learning that I possessed a piece of recondite knowledge (concerning the rules for affiliation to the Labour Party) that was essential to an article ne was writing. He himself only wrote for publication on very special occasions, but he was a wonderful instructor. When eventually he assigned me to write *Mirror* leaders, he gave me on-the-job training in composing a species of journalism in its way as perfect and complete an art form as the sonnet: a piece of writing that in 250 words explained a problem and expressed an opinion without wasting a syllable.

Cudlipp had on one occasion decided that the *Sunday Pictorial* should have a counterpart to the strange, stilted Cross-Bencher political column in the *Sunday Express* and had asked me to get together material demonstrating the extent to which Cross-bencher's frequent predictions of coming political events were erroneous. I did this, and the result was quite effective. So when I was looking for an idea for a sketch for *That Was The Week That Was*, it occurred to me that Cudlipp's notion might be turned into an ideal item for this new television series. Accordingly, the following Monday morning, I telephoned BBC Television and asked to speak to the programme's producer, Ned Sherrin, a person who until that moment was not aware I existed. To my astonishment I was instantly put through to him. I outlined my (or, actually, Cudlipp's) idea and without hesitation he commissioned a sketch based on it for his next programme.

Thus I began work on my first shooting script, which turned out not to look like a real shooting script for the simple reason that I had never actually seen a real shooting script. I typed it very carefully, in parallel black and red columns, and when it was ready Sherrin sent round a taxi for it. This very action seemed to me indescribably glamorous. At that time I had no notion that the London taxi service could not operate viably without the constant custom supplied to it by the BBC in one form or another. My sketch was transmitted on the Saturday night of that week and immediately became notorious. It consisted simply of quoted forecasts made by Cross-Bencher during recent years, together with what happened following those forecasts; in every case, of course, the prophecy had been confounded by events, and the accumulation of these incidents did make Cross-Bencher seem extremely unreliable as a seer. At that time Hugh Gaitskell, the leader of the Labour Party, was ill in hospital. At the end of the programme David Frost, the link man, picked up an advance edition of the following morning's *Sunday Express*, turned to the Cross-Bencher column, and read out a comforting prediction that Gaitskell would make a full and speedy recovery. Frost then said, leering into the camera: 'Sorry, Hugh.' Gaitskell died a few days later, and the programme's allegedly tasteless irreverence, however inadvertent in this case, was confirmed.

Hugh Cudlipp was quite peeved that I had hijacked his idea, and rebuked me in a half-hearted way, instructing me to seek specific permission if I ever wanted to write for Sherrin's programme again. Sherrin, highly pleased with my initial effort, did indeed want me to continue as a contributor; so week after week I sent in a letter of application to Lee Howard, the excellent editor of the *Mirror*.

Lee, as everyone called him, was very easy to work for, careful but casual. During my leader-writing period I used to come into the office early and, if a subject for a leader occurred to me, I would sit down and write it without consulting either Lee or Cudlipp. More often than not a better theme would be decided upon at the morning's editorial conference or would be imposed by edict from Cudlipp, who always had the final say. However, if I could get a leader accepted early, it meant that I could go home, say, at 10 p.m., rather than hang around until perhaps 2 a.m. I always had to stay until I had seen the leader right through its galley-proofed stage and sometimes even into page proof.

On one occasion I found what I thought was an excellent topical subject, related to capital punishment. I wrote what seemed to me a highly effective leader and took it down to Lee. He read it slowly, smoking one of the cigars which eventually helped to kill him. Then he looked up and said: 'This is good. But is the paper against capital punishment?' I had with great prescience brought along the cross-referenced book containing all the *Mirror*'s leaders over a considerable period, and pointed out several which denounced hanging. Lee, having found out the policy of the paper he edited, approved the leader and I got home early that night.

It was Lee, too, who asked me to pass on to Harold Wilson the best piece of advice that the Labour Leader and Prime Minister ever both received and disregarded. During the D Notices affair which destroyed Wilson's relations with the press and helped to bring down his government, Lee took me – by then a member of Wilson's staff – out to lunch at a restaurant in Chancery Lane. As we rose to take leave of each other, he said: 'Give the PM a message from me. Tell him to stop reading the newspapers.' I passed on this sage counsel, but to no avail.

Lee was not only wise but also tolerant. Week after week he condoned my moonlighting for *TW3* (as it was abbreviatedly known) by granting me written permission to write for the programme. I think, in fact, that the *Mirror* executives were quite gratified to have one of their employees making an impact in what was the most fashionable television series of the day. I continued with *That Was The Week That Was* until the BBC exterminated it, fearing that the government would take some terrible revenge on them if this programme (in which I and others lampooned most of the Ministers in the then Conservative Administration) were permitted to survive into the approaching general election campaign. The most notorious endeavour in which I was involved was a long sketch called 'The Silent Men of Westminster'. I had the idea of going through *Hansard* to check which MPs had not made any speeches whatever in recent years, and came up with a dozen or so, impartially divided between the Labour and Conservative parties. I then produced a text (still in black and red columns, even though I had seen many real, properly laid out shooting scripts by then) which pilloried these unfortunates one by one, with deleterious references to them individually and collectively. I even suggested that the Speaker of the House of Commons should be supplied with photographs of these tongue-tied parliamentarians so that he would have no trouble in recognizing them should they at any time in the future seek to catch his eye.

The following Monday, the matter was raised in Parliament on an allegation of a breach of privilege, and there were exchanges of such an imbecility that *TW3* could never have invented them. The MP who made the complaint, Sir Norman Hulbert, Conservative Member for Stockport North – one of those named in the sketch – began his remarks in the manner of a prosecuting counsel: 'On Saturday, 19th January, at approximately 10.45 p.m., the British Broadcasting Corporation televised a feature programme entitled *That Was The Week That Was*. It would appear to bear very little resemblance to any particular week. It was introduced by a Mr David Frost, who proceeded to name Right Hon. and Hon. Members . . .'

At this point, the effect of Sir Norman's remarks was somewhat impaired by cries of 'Why not?' from irreverent MPs who had to be called to order by the Speaker. The Member for Stockport North was then permitted to proceed, and went on to describe the contents of the sketch in some detail: 'I think that I can best illustrate the tenor of the remarks of Mr Frost by describing what was said about my Right Hon. friend the Member for Woodford (Sir W. Churchill) and the Hon. and highly respected Member for Liverpool Scotland (Mr Logan). This is it: "Two of them are very old men, 88-year-old Sir Winston Churchill and 91-year-old David Logan, and old men forget; they even forget the way to Westminster."'

The indictment went on relentlessly. 'Offensive remarks were made about how long it takes to mention Hon. Members' names and there was also a remark made about an Hon. Member on this side of the House and a dog.' This sounded bad, but worse was to come. 'There was, finally, a slighting reference to yourself, Mr Speaker, for it was stated that the BBC would be very pleased to supply you with the photographs of the Hon. Members referred to – the inference being that you yourself were unable to recognize them.' Sir Norman summed up: 'I submit that this performance – if one can call it so – was not only an unwarranted attack on the Hon. Members I have mentioned, but that certain suggestions were made which were really holding up the House of Commons to ridicule.'

The Speaker, promising to announce his ruling the following day, tried to get on to the next business (Gift of a Speaker's chair to the House of Representatives of Tanganyika) but certain unruly Members insisted on having their say. Reginald Paget, the Labour MP for Northampton, rose to announce that his photograph had by mistake been transmitted instead of a picture of one of the indicted MPs, and went on: 'I have communicated with the BBC to tell the Corporation that I will forgive that libel on myself since it took part in such a delightful and amusing programme.' The Speaker brushed aside this intervention, only to be confronted by Sydney Silverman, Labour MP for Nelson and Colne, who asked 'whether it would be a breach of privilege on the part of this admirable programme to include this incident in its programme next week?' The Speaker huffily responded: 'My powers in the matter do not extend to a cognate question of such a kind.' Next day, however, he proved himself an outstanding occupant of his office by dismissing Sir Norman's complaint out of hand, pausing only to allow the last word to the voluble Mr Silverman: 'Most Hon. Members would infinitely rather be asked why they do not speak than why they do.'

Sir Norman, defeated in one arena, immediately took up the fight directly with the BBC. He demanded an apology from the Corporation, pointing out that he was a member of the panel of Chairmen who presided over Commons' standing committees, and claiming that he was accordingly debarred from taking part in debates. The BBC, who had gloried in the publicity this episode had provided, now got cold feet and asked me what was to be done. I spent several days studying *Hansard* and compiled a dossier showing that, during the period when Sir Norman had remained mute, all the other members of the Chairmen's Panel had made numerous speeches, indeed some of them (and in particular a Mr George Thomas) finding it almost impossible to refrain from uttering for as much as a day at a time. Consequently, the following events occurred: the BBC triumphantly told Sir Norman to get lost; they paid me a fee not only for the sketch but another for the research; they conceived a most heartening faith in my accuracy as a contributor and commissioned even more work from me; and in the 1964 election the Stockport North Labour Party used my material in their election campaign and succeeded in unseating poor Sir Norman.

TW3 was followed by a pallid successor, coyly named *Not So Much a Programme More A Way of Life*, which spread over all three nights of the weekend and, as well as sketches, included the BBC's first attempt at a chat show. I went on writing sketches and was, for a time, one of the members of the team of conversationalists. I did not prove a success in my latter role partly, no doubt, because of my personal inadequacies but also due to the influence of Donald Baverstock, the voluble and agreeable controller of the whole enterprise. At the dinner regularly held before the programme, Baverstock used to put me into such a muddle that I had no idea what I was saying when we went on the air.

Ned Sherrin, however, retained faith in my abilities and asked me to write a whole programme for him called *ABC of Britain*. This major event (for me, if not for viewers) starred Gordon Jackson who, after the inspiration of speaking my lines, inevitably went on to become a TV superstar in *Upstairs, Downstairs*. I provided a collection of sketches, and was permitted to write one about the cinema. I had read in a film magazine that the actor-writer-director Bryan Forbes had complained that continental film-makers were given too much modish attention in this country, and that it was about time that a British director was made the subject of a cult. I therefore devised a dialogue involving a committed Forbes admirer who, to show his allegiance, wore a badge inscribed with the initials BF. The climax came when, after an exchange of views concerning the procedure for launching a Bryan Forbes cult, the camera cut to a Man in the Street who declared: 'I don't know what all this BF nonsense is about. I've been calling Bryan Forbes a cult for years.'

My work for *TW3* had been noted by those with the patience to peer at the roller caption which ended the programme, and on which the names of most of the population of Britain seemed to be inscribed in strict alphabetical order. As a result I was approached by a newly established satirical nightclub – actually called, I believe, the Satire – which invited me to write topical lyrics for songs to be performed there. I knew nothing whatever about lyric-writing, though I had affirmed often enough in my film reviews, when flailing an unsuccessful musical, that it was a skilled craft; and I had certainly never acquired the skill. All the same, I was ready to try anything and I therefore sat down and composed what amounted to, or at any rate sought to be, comic verse. I did not know how to write words to be sung, and I was never put in touch with the composer of the music, assuming there was such a person. The product of my labours was a collection of doggerel of which I had the grace not to be proud. My attempts to be smartly humorous consisted of tortured puns which matched Cousins (the surname of the then General Secretary of the Transport Workers' Union) and Brothers (the mode of fraternal address within trade unions).

The proprietors of the night club seemed quite pleased, to the extent indeed of handing over to me a small but not absolutely negligible sum of money, with an invitation to attend at the Satire one night to hear my work performed. Wary of what I might find when I got there, I decided to make the trip to Mayfair on my own. I was prepared to experience humiliation, but not to have it witnessed. I need not have worried. I stumbled down into a kind of basement and found myself one of a handful of people, too few really even to be sitting around in a desultory fashion. I was provided with a drink and positioned myself in a corner, pretending not really to be there at all while awaiting the moment when the cabaret would start and, with it, my moment of release. I finished my drink, and continued to wait. After a prolonged period, during which a pianist filled in what would have been gaps in the conversation had there been any conversation, I did not notice any signs of preparation for the cabaret and therefore left. I do not know whether my songs were performed that evening or in fact ever, but from that night onward Stephen Sondheim was able to live free from fear of serious competition.

Then at last I was given my big chance, the nearest I would ever get to what could be regarded as the opportunity to write the screenplay for a major movie. Through an intermediary, Birds

Eye Foods approached me. They wanted me to provide material for a short film which could be shown to an audience composed of their company's salesmen, the idea being that I should galvanize them through laughter into swelling the sales of the various packaged products that lay awaiting customers in grocery iceboxes. It was not to be a movie in the sense that actors would speak lines and display emotions. Rather, it was to be a sophisticated form of magic lantern show, with images of an exceptionally simple kind and accompanying words which would transform the event if not into art then at any rate into some form of entertainment. Once again I went to work, and was able to produce yet another collection of sheets of paper with black and red parallel sections.

This was accepted and transformed into material regarded as suitable for exhibition, and I was asked to a building near Fetter Lane to share the experience with the massed salesmen. They watched attentively, presumably since they were there on the company's time and therefore in a sense being paid to watch. However, no one seemed to have told them in advance that what they were to see would be funny, and they failed to pick up the idea for themselves. This reaction might have been due to the nature of the material they witnessed. They sat there in decent and respectful silence, not coughing very much and not laughing at all. I came to the conclusion that persuading others to sell fish fingers with zealous dedication was no laughing matter. After this event the fortunes of Birds Eye Foods prospered exceedingly, this success possibly having no connection with my efforts to enthuse the salesmen, though equally possibly resulting from a determination by the salesmen to prove that they could sell cod fillets without being compulsorily amused into it. That was the first and only time when work of mine reached the big cinema screen.

I remained enthralled not only by watching films but by information about how they were made. Although I continued to read the fan magazines *Picturegoer* and *Picture Show*, and went on doing so until they expired along with the mass cinema audience, I was anxious to have access to more profound cinema journalism. The British Film Institute published an impressively intellectual quarterly named *Sight and Sound* which was so unreadable that its credentials for seriousness were unchallenged, together with a *Monthly Film Bulletin* which contained full details of every film licensed (rather like a dog that had to be placed under restraint) by the Board of Trade. I obtained these periodicals as part of my subscription to the BFI.

I then discovered a squat little publication, issued in New York, called *Films in Review*, and sent an international money order (at that time a laborious process, involving filling in numerous forms to comply with exchange control and requiring the payment of a fee rather larger than the amount of money to be sent) to obtain a regular subscription. The magazine began arriving monthly, or at any rate approximately monthly, since there were months when it bafflingly failed to appear. Perusing its glossy little pages, I found myself at last among people even madder about films than myself. There were articles describing in fanatical detail the careers of persons whose place in the cinema was so transitory and minimal that I had never heard of them at all. There were letters from correspondents correcting errors of the most minute kind contained in such articles. There were more letters requesting information of a recondite nature about the whereabouts of obscure performers of the past. There were further letters in which readers, for the delectation of other readers, set quizzes about the cinema so perplexing that I felt knowledgeable if I could answer correctly as many as one question. There were additional letters denouncing the inaccuracy of questions, or answers, or both, in previous quizzes.

Nothing, however recondite, escaped the beady eyes of the readers of *Films in Review*. Paul Frederick Johnson of Minneapolis wrote sharply to the editor in October 1957: 'In *Helen of Troy* Rosanna Podesta's vaccination mark shines in the dusky light while she and Jacques Sernas hide in the brush from Greek soldiers. When John Wayne inspects the arrow of rocks left by an Indian woman in *The Searchers*, he wears two different pairs of shoes. In one shot the shoes are brown, in another they are a brown and white combination. In the opening shot of *Heaven Knows, Mr Allison* – Robert Mitchum on a raft – Mitchum's hair is wet. In the next shot it is dry. The shade of Lauren Bacall's lipstick darkens in *Written on the Wind* without her having applied any new.'

In the August–September 1965 issue, Robert Rosterman of Chicago supplied information that no movie enthusiast could possibly do without: 'Practically everyone knows Anne Shirley and Gig Young took those names from characters they portrayed in films, but few realize that veteran actress Minerva Urecal

113

invented that name from the syllabic sounds of her birthplace: Eureka, California.' Reader Rosterman concluded, unanswerably: 'Her real name is Holer.'

Everyone who had anything published in the pages of *Films in Review* seemed to be motivated by mania, and sometimes by sheer hatred: of films, soundtrack music, stars, supporting players and, especially, other readers of the magazine. Most obsessive of all were the reviews of movies themselves, which would ignore themes, performances, camerawork and all other ingredients by which I had been accustomed to judge a picture, and would instead go into a tantrum about some tiny aspect, perhaps of continuity or titling. After a time reviewers, obviously on instructions, commenced to classify films on aggregates of percentages, the basis of which was never comprehensibly explained, thus: '*Unfaithfully Yours* E–2%; G–40%; F–43%; P–15%.' Those daunting statistics could, of course, have referred to the outdoor temperature when the film was being shown, possibly excluding the windchill factor.

I always read *Films in Review* with care and, if I could not summon up respect, then at any rate with ungrudging admiration for the commitment of those whose lives seemed to revolve around it. My attitude to the British monthly *Films and Filming* was from the start one of scorn. Published by a group which, similarly uniting noun and gerund, owned a whole batch of monthlies covering (after a fashion) various other arts, *Films and Filming* was a would-be intellectual magazine compiled by people who would not have known an intellectual if they had fallen over one in Buckingham Palace Road where the office of the parent company, Hansom Books, was situated. This was manned with almost unique incompetence, which led to massive confusion about subscriptions combined with an inability to put things right. As the years passed *Films and Filming* gradually changed. Its pages, and then its cover, seemed gradually to become dominated by photographs of brawny young men dressed in very little if anything, and the classified advertisements, previously filled with plaintive requests for old stills of faded stars, began to be monopolized by pleas from young men who wished to meet other young men. The police must have stepped in, because before very long the classifieds were once again concerned with demands for pictures of Shirley Temple in *Baby Take a Bow*. In the end the proprietor of all of these magazines, having apparently got himself into a frightful financial pickle, died, leaving me, who had remained faithful to *Films and Filming* – as to *Films in Review* – through all its vicissitudes and eccentricities, with an uncompleted subscription.

There was a time not so long ago when very few books about films were published in Britain apart from *Picture Show* and *Picturegoer* annuals and other works of a devotional nature. One day, when in London on one of my visits for a job interview, I had looked in on Collet's bookshop on Charing Cross Road, the one that later was to specialize in selling Penguin publications but which at that time stocked a bit of everything, including second-hand volumes. Glancing idly along the shelves (I can remember exactly where: on the left-hand side wall, about two thirds along and about three-quarters up from the floor) I came upon two volumes with the bewitching titles of *Screen World 1952* and *Screen World 1953*. I seized both of them and, looking inside, found that they were the books of my dreams. Each one contained full credit titles for all the films released in the United States the previous year, together with photographic illustrations. There was a section devoted to foreign films, British pictures coming under that heading, and the books, edited by a benefactor of mankind by the name of Daniel Blum, were rounded off with various special features and appendices, including, curiously, Portrait Doll facsimiles of prominent stars as well as pictures of Promising Newcomers. These *Screen World* annuals cost, respectively, 16s. and 30s. apiece, which was more than I could afford in my unemployed state but for which I was lucky to have in my pocket sufficient ready money to meet the price. I paid up with trembling hand and spent the journey back to Leeds gloating over my trophies.

My aim in life was to obtain the missing volumes, a project in which, with the aid of friends in America, I succeeded. From then on, I bought each new issue as it came out, which it did year after year, the series even surviving the death of Daniel Blum, who fell in active service to the cinema. The new editor, John Willis, brought in changes which included ditching the Portrait Dolls, which in a way I regretted, but involved an additional section providing the true names of the stars. From this I learned that June Allyson was actually Ella Geisman and the apparently exotic May Britt really May Britt Wilkins, that the glamorous Lana Turner had been prosaically christened Mildred, and that to

her parents Cyd Charisse, the girl with the longest legs in Hollywood, would always be Tula Ellice Finklea.

My rapturous discovery of *Screen World* galvanized me into
searching bookshops for further revelations. None could equal
that, but occasionally I would find other, kindred volumes, and
these soon filled enough shelf space to form the modest nucleus of
a film library. The first bookshop in London I came upon that
specialized in works about the cinema was Zwemmer's, situated
on Charing Cross Road a little above Collet's. Zwemmer's was
mainly devoted to works about art and architecture but set aside
space for books about the cinema on a table and a few shelves in a
cranny off its main premises. Then friends in New York told me
of a shop in that city with the pretentious yet irresistible name of
Cinemabilia so, when the first opportunity arose, I went there. It
was situated ambiguously in that part of New York where
Greenwich Village meets the Bowery, and I was able to get there
from mid-town Manhattan by bus, thus avoiding the terrors of
the subway.

The place was scarcely welcoming. It was not exactly dingy,
but it gave off an air of profound seediness. The stock was laid out
on (or perhaps flung on to) various tables, or pushed untidily in a
not easily comprehensible fashion on to shelves, some of them far
from accessible. The staff seemed surly to the point where they
appeared ready to inflict some sort of punishment on any would-
be customer with the effrontery to ask a question. I later found
that this unwelcoming attitude, together with an untidiness verging
on squalor, was typical of many (if not all) bookshops specializing
in the movies, some of these shops being redolent with cats'
urine. Perhaps the idea was to test the determination – and
therefore the sincerity – of patrons. If so, I qualified without
question, since not only did I buy several volumes and return in
future years to go on buying more, but I even had myself placed
on Cinemabilia's mailing list, an esoteric but indispensable document for any literate cineman.

Books were one way of obtaining a permanent record of films I
had seen, especially if screenplays could be obtained, such as
James Agee's script for the intimidating *The Night of the Hunter*.
Another form of memento was long-playing records, and I therefore decided to invest in a Boots record-player, this being the type
enthusiastically recommended by Edward Greenfield, a music
critic of the *Guardian*, all of whose recommendations of anything

were enthusiastic to the extent that he was once described as 'a beserk cement-mixer' but most of whose recommendations were highly reliable, as indeed, the Boots equipment turned out to be.

This was long before nostalgia record shops began to burgeon all over the place, and a search for movie soundtracks therefore had to be a hit-and-miss quest in run-of-the-mill establishments. Most of these contained Films and Shows sections where discs of current releases were available. However, what I was really after was records of older films I had enjoyed. On visits to Leeds I found that a shop named Barkers, in which served sturdy Yorkshire ladies who stood no nonsense, was highly reliable. In London, far and away the best was Gamages, that strange department store situated on Holborn just opposite the multicoloured skyscraper to which the *Daily Mirror* had moved. This shop was located on several levels not easily accessible from each other, a structural characteristic superficially the consequence of expansion from one building to another but in my firm view the result of a plan by the proprietors to make shopping more exciting and unpredictable. Gamages contained a record department which few but me seemed to visit and which, as a result, had a slightly shopworn stock of venerable age. There was also a 'second hand' box which was regularly augmented.

Here I swooped with glee on recordings of Minnelli's *Kismet* and of the sound track of *Some Like It Hot*, featuring Marilyn Monroe breathing rather than singing a lyric entitled 'I Wanna Be Loved By You'. On one auspicious day I came upon a treasurable rarity, Donen's *Funny Face*; and though I never could then, and never did afterwards, find the soundtrack of Quine's *My Sister Eileen*, I did discover a recording of the Broadway cast of Leonard Bernstein's stage musical based on the same story, *Wonderful Town*, with marvellous songs of which the most fetching was Rosalind Russell suggesting 'One Hundred Easy Ways to Lose A Man'. This unexpected find led me to expand my range some-what, and as a result, as second-best to a soundtrack that seemed not to exist, I bought a record of another Bernstein-Comden-Green musical, the theatrical forerunner of the movie *On the Town*. Mostly the records I bought were of musicals but I unearthed one containing several speeches from the soundtrack of MGM's *Julius Caesar* and bought another of the music by the Modern Jazz Quartet playing for the wonderfully atmospheric thriller set in a fogbound Venice, *Sait-on Jamais?*

A corner of my sitting-room therefore began to be filled with cinematographic icons of one kind and another. These mementoes, however, proved insufficient to content my cravings. If film-making could not come to me, I would go to it. Partly by design, partly by accident, from the 1950s onwards I began to make my way to locations where films were being shot. I had become a committed admirer of the adaptations of Edgar Allan Poe's stories directed by Roger Corman, later to become a cult film producer but at the outset of his career an artificer of movies made on a shoestring. I had gone to see his first effort in this genre, *The Fall of the House of Usher*, at the Compton Cinema Club, a small basement auditorium where, for good reasons or bad, I felt (on the occasions that I visited it) that I would at any moment be arrested for a crime I was not aware I had committed.

Corman followed this first essay with others, including *The Pit and the Pendulum* and *The Premature Burial*. All could be relied upon to offer Vincent Price, who was liable to end up as viscous liquid or worse, and a standing set of a haunted mansion, complete with echoing corridors, secret passages, and a built-in crypt for easy access to family skeletons. There were also always a good many red candles, which I came to call Price's candles, chosen for their photogenic qualities rather than their sanguinary associations. The supporting casts were filled with vapid heroines and heroes, the latter including a young and innocent Jack Nicholson presumably picking up tips ready for when he would be the main star in Stanley Kubrick's glossy horror show, *The Shining*.

Corman (unwisely in my view, since I really was happily at home in that crypt) transferred operations to England. Here he directed *The Masque of the Red Death*, which I gladly recognized as a satire on Bergman's *The Seventh Seal*, but whose Black Mass sequences had been savagely cut by a censor who feared that picturegoers might be inspired to rush out and desecrate churches. Now I heard that Corman was at it again, on location for another Poe venture, *The Tomb of Ligeia*, so I hurried off to Castle Acre Priory in Norfolk to watch him at work. His activities were impeded by a crowd of sightseeing visitors who could not legally be kept away, since the priory was a Ministry of Works responsibility. Furthermore a cat, essential to the scene being filmed, ran away, and messengers had to be sent to the nearest village to rent another. During the afternoon I spent there not much work was done – towards a prologue which, complete with cat, turned out to be really quite frightening – but in the middle of a cemetery I did have the opportunity of long conversations with Vincent Price about his moonlighting job as an art-buyer for Sears Roebuck.

This first experience of location shooting suggested to me that filming was a very tedious pursuit unless you were a technician, and this was confirmed to me subsequently in Israel on as many as three separate occasions. I was a regular visitor to the Land of the Bible, but speedily exhausted its scriptural associations. Its cinematic possibilities seemed potentially much more fruitful, and so it proved. While in the north of the country I was told that a big scene was to be shot in a modern adaptation of the Judith and Holofernes story from the Bible, Sophia Loren being the Judith of the movie's title. Much of a specially built kibbutz was to be deliberately burned down, and I was invited to the incineration. I found that I was not the only spectator. The site was thronged with visitors from neighbouring real kibbutzim, who examined the structures in minute detail and, as is the way with Israelis and especially with kibbutzniks, criticized what was being done in every particular and offered suggestions for improvement. These, however, were to no avail, since the entire enterprise was enveloped in confusion of a kind which to me it did not seem could possibly be sorted out, a judgement which turned out to be accurate since, although I was there for several hours, not a foot of film was exposed. The production company, Paramount, might in the end have wished that this state of affairs had prevailed, since the film, when completed, lacked both artistic merit and commercial success, despite the fact that I, to see what came of it all in the end, misguidedly bought a ticket.

On another occasion, being driven along a minor road not far from Jerusalem, I suddenly thought I saw Yul Brynner sitting on a chair in the middle of a field, looking fed up. I therefore asked the driver to stop, and went and had a look, and did indeed find Yul Brynner sitting alone in a field not only looking fed up but being fed up. What we were watching was another episode in the agonized filming of a desperate effort called *Cast a Giant Shadow*, and Mr Brynner was waiting for the film's producers to make up their minds what to do next, which they never in fact did, although they went on shooting for want of something else to do.

My next and final visit to an Israeli location was carefully arranged in advance with the film's production unit. Norman Jewison, who had presumably been given permission to film in

119

the country because the authorities had drawn inaccurate con-
clusions from his surname, was shooting part of *Jesus Christ
Superstar* on a hillside on the occupied West Bank. On this
particular day he was seeking to simulate day-for-night conditions,
employing for the purpose various devices, no doubt of massive
technical complexity, which looked like white parasols and
enormous sheets of silver kitchen foil. It was very hot indeed,
which certainly assisted the young actor playing Jesus (a person
by the name of Ted Neeley who despite, or more likely because
of, having performed in this film, emphatically did not go on to
stardom) in looking tormented, as required, while he toiled again
and again up a hillside singing a dolesome ditty.

Much the most dramatic event of the day came at the lunch
break. This being technically a British product, union rules
required a certain standard of catering to which, it appeared,
Israeli cuisine could not attain. A mobile canteen had therefore
been brought out from, I think, Acton, and now commenced to
dispense lunches to the large numbers of people who were required
to implant on celluloid the agonies of Christ. There was, no doubt
also as a result of union regulations, a choice of menu, one of the
main dishes being pork, which I judged in the circumstances to
be an insensitive decision. That I was completely wrong was
demonstrated by the rush to the pork counter of every Israeli
employed on the film crew in a technical capacity, these renegades
being determined to take advantage of what might be a unique
opportunity to taste forbidden fruit.

When I could not attach myself to the unit of a film currently
being made on location, I made it my business, when travelling
abroad, to visit places which had at a former time been locations
for films I had seen. In Bavaria I visited one of the castles built at
Neuschwanstein for King Ludwig, which were used extensively
in Visconti's screen biography. So extravagant was this edifice
that I got the feeling that the Mad King really had intended it as a
film set rather than as a private home. In New York I went out by
boat to the Statue of Liberty and, as I clambered around it,
thought not so much of its message of hope and inspiration to
huddled immigrants as of the climactic chase for which it formed
a monster adventure playground in Hitchcock's *Saboteur*. In
Venice I traced the very canal bank from which Katharine
Hepburn had fallen during *Summer Madness*, an experience which
had a permanent effect on her since the pollution of the water

caused her eyes ever after to water, and was principally responsible for the tearful nature of her performance in *Guess Who's Coming to Dinner*.

My folly reached its peak during another visit to the United States when, having visited the Petrified Forest in the film of that name (Humphrey Bogart, Bette Davis) and walked along the Santa Fe Trail (Errol Flynn) which, despite its remote and romantic name, was filled mainly with antique shops, art galleries and ice cream parlours, I made my way across a desert to a tiny spot named Lamy. The connection between this place and a film was tenuous: it contained a functioning station of the Atchison, Topeka and Santa Fe railroad, and I thought this might contain some redolence of the superb number sung by Judy Garland in *The Harvey Girls*, even though I knew that the number had been shot on a sound stage at MGM. I had, as it happened, met some Harvey Girls, since the Fred Harvey company, which stemmed from the original Harvey enterprise featured in the picture, seemed to have won a monopolistic concession for souvenir shops at all National Parks in the Far West, and I had been to a good number of these. These Harvey Girls were not, however, glamorous and melodious along the lines of the film. Watching these comfortable, plump matrons as they tirelessly exhibited informative T-shirts and ethnic key-rings for potential customers, I got the feeling that all they could sing, if pressed, would be hymns of a militant kind which they had learned as part of the routine of becoming born-again Christians which all of them, judging by dress and demeanour, were.

I arrived at Lamy to find that it consisted almost solely of the railway station itself, which disappointingly was operated by a computer but which had been built (in 1882) with lavish use of multi-coloured tiles and marble, even – or perhaps especially – in the public conveniences. It was equipped with hand-carved wooden benches which had once furnished the lobby of an hotel next door and, apart from the computer, was everything that a Wild West railway station could be expected to be.

To attain my cinematic objective I was not above trespassing, if need be. In Salzburg I decided to see as many as possible of the sites featured in the film *The Sound of Music*, a film sentimental to the last possible degree, which all my intellectual judgements told me was inadequate to my elevated tastes but which whenever I saw it (for I viewed it several times) caused me against my will to break out in passionate sobs. I inspected the elaborate decorated fountain which is featured in a key scene, though I was distracted by shouts of 'Hit! Hit!' which, upon investigation, turned out to be cries of recognition for Edward Heath, the former British Prime Minister, who was spied by alert Austrians crossing the road to the opera house, there to share an elevating experience with an audience which, to my critical eye, seemed to consist of ageing ex-members of the Hitler Youth.

I very much wanted to see the pretty, delicate garden pavilion in which the podgy young man who in the film's plot did turn out to be a member of the Hitler Youth had sung 'Sixteen Going on Seventeen' with one of the numerous Trapp children. I tracked it to a Salzburg suburb but found on arrival that not only was it in the grounds of a private house but that this private house was being used as a college housing large numbers of healthy girls who seemed mostly to come from Texas. Not at this late stage prepared to be thwarted of my objective, I walked boldly in, ready if necessary to pretend that I was some sort of instructor of a nature that could not exactly be specified. However, these young women seemed to be so preoccupied with their own affairs, none of them obviously educational, that I was able without hindrance to look around until I found the pavilion. It sat on a lawn next to a lake, rather forlorn, with broken window-panes and an embellishment of cobwebs, but it had been seen and could, having been suitably photographed, be struck from my list.

Much less exotic were the locations that I visited in Britain. While addressing, in my political capacity, a meeting of the National Union of Public Employees in Hyde Town Hall, in what used to be Cheshire before local government reform dismembered that inoffensive county, I suddenly recognized that this pleasing and elaborate interior had been used for the climactic and ultimately disorderly palais-de-danse sequence in John Schlesinger's *Yanks*. This realization caused me to falter in some rather complex remarks about grant-related expenditure assessments. On my mental checklist I was ticking off yet another location to add to my private collection.

9

CLOSE-UP

I saw where films had been made. I met some of those who appeared in them. Quite a deal of the time, these encounters turned out badly. I discovered that it was difficult for me to find sensible questions to put to my idols. All I really wanted to do was to have a look at her or him, see how they measured up to their screen image, possibly cadge an autograph, and then depart starry-eyed. However, I found that an encounter could not be tidily stage-managed in this way. After all, the idols could not simply stand or sit there looking like an idol. Sometimes, indeed, the idol did not look at all like an idol, but was much smaller than expected or had a spotty face or even a running nose. Such flaws could only lead to disillusion. I learned, further, that the idol, on his or her part, also had a problem about how to behave. How were sensible answers to be given to foolish questions? Maybe, in any case, the idol was too stupid to give sensible answers even to sensible questions. Maybe the idol wished he or she had never consented to the meeting in the first place.

Such embarrassments were undoubtedly my fault, since I should have learned from a bruising episode endured in my late teens. I had conceived an unreasoning (although perfectly reasonable) adoration for the actress-comedienne Dora Bryan, especially for her performance as a Lancashire lass of easy virtue but impressive and abusive persistence in Robert Donat's film of *The Cure for Love*. I admired the artful way in which, in her croaky voice, she delivered lines that on paper would have seemed banal. As the tart in *The Fallen Idol* who tried to help the ambassador's son who had run away from a murder and ended up in a police station, she delivered the prostitute's stock invitation, 'Would you like to come home with me?' in a smirking way which disgusted watching constables but actually won the confidence of the child. In another picture (*13 East Street*, I think) she provided a vivid description of her husband as victim of a severe electric shock administered by a household implement: 'Before you could say Jack Robinson, he was flat on his back with a blue light running up and down him!'

Overwhelmed by a timid yet consuming passion for this paragon, and hearing that she was to appear in a revue at the Opera House in Manchester, I wrote and asked if she would receive me and was staggered to receive a positive response. On the appointed afternoon I attended the matinée performance and then, all a-tremble, made my way to the stage door, was granted entrance, and was directed to Miss Bryan's dressing-room. I knocked and she answered. I explained who I was, and an expression of bewilderment crossed her face. I realized that she had completely forgotten that I was coming. However, with a good (if somewhat ruffled) grace she admitted me, and I did my best to express my sentiments in eloquent tones. I had not got very far – though, I am sure, more than far enough for her – when the door opened and there entered a man who to me seemed on terms of excessive familiarity with the star. He even kissed her. My instinct was to knock him down, but I was wise enough not to express my outraged feelings in this way. This was just as well, since the offending intruder turned out to be one Bill Lawton, a Lancashire league cricketer and Miss Bryan's secret (or at any rate secret from me) fiancé, soon to be her husband. I left in haste, jealousy and chagrin.

I did not, however, absorb the salutary lesson that I should have learned from this dreadful fiasco, and in later years went on seeking to meet entertainers I admired.

When in Israel for the filming of *Judith*, I was granted a personal interview at the Dan-Carmel Hotel in Haifa by the portrayer of the title role, Sophia Loren. Our conversation was innocuous to the point of vapidity, but I was able to see for myself that she was, when observed in three dimensions from only a yard or two away, even more beautiful than I had previously thought. I came away an even more besotted admirer. This was not the outcome of an encounter with another actress whom I had admired at least as much, Lauren Bacall, after whom I had yearned ever since *The Big Sleep*. I met her at a party given at his palace in Chelsea by Lord Weidenfeld. This was not long after the resignation of President Nixon and, since Bacall was known as a politically committed person, I endeavoured to discuss this matter with her. She brushed me off after about two sentences, which of course she had every right to do, even though, looking around the room, I could not for the life of me see anyone more interesting to talk to than myself. Later I forgave her, and went to see her in the musical *Woman of the Year* on Broadway. However, when I read in the papers that she had been rude to her successor in the role, Raquel Welch, I was more than ready to believe it.

During the time I was employed at Downing Street, I myself was responsible for the presence at another party of Ginger Rogers. Harold Wilson had endowed the phrase 'political party' with a new meaning. He had come to the conclusion that overseas statesmen, conferring with him on visits to this country and eligible for official entertainment, did not especially relish meeting senior civil servants, important but dull industrialists, and the various other special brands of faceless if sometimes worthy people who had up to then automatically been included in guest lists compiled for the genteel and soporific receptions which followed more restricted official dinners in the large state guest rooms at No. 10. Wilson accordingly decided to give foreign prime ministers and presidents the chance to meet Britons they had actually heard of, including sportsmen, especially footballers, and indoor entertainers as well.

I was offered the opportunity of adding to the guest lists for these occasions a number of persons from the world of the stage and the cinema; and Downing Street soon became known as the place where you could meet the likes of Tom Courtenay or Paul Scofield over a glass of sherry. I even smuggled in Dora Bryan, despite having acquired the bitter knowledge that she was a supporter of the Conservative Party. When the rather dreadful musical *Mame* arrived at Drury Lane, I determined to lure to Downing Street the star of the show, Ginger Rogers, and was gratified when she accepted the invitation.

As all film stars should she turned up dressed in a garment which looked as though it had cost thousands of dollars and had provided employment for dozens of seamstresses. She was by then getting along somewhat in years and looked, it had to be admitted, a mite pudgy about the face and no longer as sylphlike as in *Follow the Fleet*. However, there was a sparkle in her eyes that gave evidence of the true Ginger Rogers definitely being present somewhere inside, and I hastened to converse with her. Unlike Lauren Bacall she was pleasant and forthcoming, and still capable of giving a star performance even in what became, in the crush that was developing as guests continued to arrive, a heavily populated crowd scene.

I was perfectly ready to spend much of the rest of the evening listening to this agreeable lady's memories about the old days at RKO and suchlike, but I felt that she would prefer to have the chance of meeting others besides a nobody such as myself. In addition, as an auxiliary host, I had the duty of mingling with other guests and making sure they had enough to drink. I therefore excused myself, confident that Ginger Rogers would soon be the centre of an admiring throng. No doubt she would have been, had people known who she was. Unfortunately, she was not immediately recognizable as the graceful and lissome girl whom Astaire had whirled around in 'Cheek to Cheek' and, when a little later on she came into my view, I was shocked to see that she had only her husband, no doubt an extremely pleasant man, talking to her. I therefore myself went to speak to her again, but got the feeling that she had run out of things to say to me and accordingly scurried about rustling up other companions for her. Throughout the evening I kept on having to do this, but abandoned the endeavour when I noticed that her husband had seen what I was up to and obviously felt that his wife was too important to have to be rescued by the likes of me. Ginger Rogers's visit to London, which lasted fifty-six weeks, was a triumphant commercial success, but it has to be admitted that her evening at Downing Street was a social disaster.

When Frank Sinatra came to call there, no one had any difficulty in recognizing him and he was not at all short of people to talk to. He arrived surrounded by a small group of tough-looking men – himself, having put on weight and a threatening demeanour since his rather weedy early days on the screen, certainly being no milksop – all of whom could have won roles from Central Casting as either gangsters or racecourse touts. I was given the job of steering him into the room and, while not myself ever having been sufficient of an admirer as to wish to monopolize him, took the opportunity of a word or two. His songwriter, Sammy Kahn, had recently been in London giving his clever stage show, and I mentioned this to Sinatra who responded with an apparently derogatory remark about Kahn which might have been affectionate and jocular but, on the other hand, might not. He was then swept away from me, and thus ended my friendship with the legendary star, who at least did not get any of his entourage to beat me up, and who made no attempt to write any letters – unlike Robert Kennedy who, on his sole visit to No. 10, immediately sat down outside the Cabinet Room and commenced to catch up with his correspondence on the Prime Minister's stationery.

I was myself the beneficiary of counterpart entertainment at the White House, during the tenures of both Presidents Johnson and Nixon. Under President Johnson's regime I had lunch with him in his private apartments, a meal whose smooth flow was adversely affected by the intermittent attention paid by the President to numerous television sets tuned to different channels. Dinner at the White House was not a gourmet's delight, but it was an experience worth remembering if not precisely memorable. Conversation was assisted, or hindered, whichever way you prefer to look at it, by a bevy of violinists, known, I believe, as the Strolling Strings of the United States Air Force. Their role was to wander around the room, insinuating themselves between tables, treating each batch of guests to a snatch of itinerant music, and turning themselves into a clean-limbed, close-cropped version of Hungarian fiddlers. During the Johnson dinner their attentions constituted an unwelcome interruption, since I shared a table with two interesting celebrities: Linda Bird, the President's daughter, and Jim Backus, the voice of the short-sighted, bumbling Mr Magoo in the delightful UPA cartoons.

This pair dominated the table and, though they had little or nothing to say to me, their own conversation was absorbing enough, Linda Bird demonstrating herself to be more than a match for Backus when it came to Hollywood gossip and Backus himself frequently lapsing into his Mr Magoo voice, this apparently being an uncontrollable spasm on his part. The evening was scarcely elevating, but at any rate was a definite experience. At the Nixon dinner I glimpsed Greer Garson in the distance, but no one thought me worth introducing to her. Instead, at the lowly table where I was placed, I was totally surrounded by Middle-Western Congressmen and their wives, all of whom concentrated on a thorough discussion of the educational shortcomings of their children together with deleterious references to persons of another colour. As their endless harsh, intolerant, small-minded drone went on, I began to long for another visit from the Strolling Strings. I have no knowledge of whether this conversation, held during the Nixon era, was taped but, if so, I have nothing to worry about since no one invited me – or even gave me the chance – to contribute a single word.

It was at the National Film Theatre in London that I had my brief but, to me memorable encounter with Gene Kelly. I met him at a reception. He was by then aged 67. He was considerably stouter than in his great days on the screen, but his voice sounded exactly the same, light yet husky, and with the trace of a permanent cold in the nose. He removed a piece of chewing gum from his mouth in order to look respectable for television, but was steadfastly refusing to hold court, instead choosing to sit in an anteroom with a French woman friend who might have been an older version of the Nina Foch who so much fancied him in *An American in Paris*. He did, however, mingle sufficiently to consent to autograph for me a copy of the screenplay of *Singin' in the Rain* with the flattering flourish 'To GK from GK', and he did draw aside the veil to reveal with unparalleled candour the hitherto closely guarded secrets behind the filming of the title number of *Singin' in the Rain*. He disclosed that the initial preparations consisted of a decision that 'It's going to be raining and I'm going to be singing'. He offered the astounding information that it was 'an easy number to do except that it was very wet'.

At a press conference he was much more forthcoming, except when asked (by me) how he and Stanley Donen had shared their responsibilities in the three films they had directed together. I had expected a detailed account of this productive association, but instead Kelly dismissed Donen's activities almost totally, implying that his collaborator had simply acted as some sort of minor assistant, if not actually having had responsibility only for bringing the tea. By then, however, I had recognized that film stars could not be relied upon to appear or behave as they did on screen – quite certainly fortunately in the case of Vincent Price – and that most of them were relatively shy people who knew how to do one thing, and quite often one thing only, with varying degrees of efficiency. When it came to conversation they did not set themselves up as rivals to Isaiah Berlin.

Vincente Minnelli as a conversationalist did not even set himself up as a rival to the man who read out the bulletins during the Falklands War. I had first gone to see him when he was in London in 1962 for the opening of his re-make of *The Four Horsemen of the Apocalypse*, an unqualified disaster as he was the first to acknowledge. When I was admitted to the Harlequin Suite at the Dorchester (where I had come to interview him for a weekly publication called *Time and Tide*, for which I wrote as a freelance during the 1960s) I nevertheless found him – garbed in a black velvet dressing-gown with the initials VM in red on the breast pocket, and yellow pyjamas – playing over the records of the soundtrack music, perhaps as some kind of dirge. I was admitted by a buxom young Yugoslav lady who turned out to be (but I am afraid did not remain for long) his third wife, and it was a good thing she was there since without her it would almost have been impossible to keep any kind of talk going.

Minnelli was both pleasant and welcoming but, frustratingly, at best semi-articulate, as was proved some years later by a lecture he gave at the National Film Theatre which consisted mainly of silence. On that occasion he did display a sense of humour. I was wearing a surgical collar for a disc ailment and, upon the renewal of our acquaintance, he greeted me with the words, 'Father O'Connor, I presume'. At our earlier meeting as at our later encounter, he was slim, balding, almost ethereal in appearance, and very intellectual-looking, indeed, a judgement envinced by the visual beauty of his work though not by his demeaning book of memoirs – ghosted, I very much trust – called *I Remember It Well*. However, when we talked at the Dorchester, prodded or possibly even stimulated by my blatantly sycophantic admiration, he did provide a certain amount of information. He had hated making *Kismet*, operetta not being his 'kind of thing'. His favourite actors to work with with were first Kirk Douglas, second, Spencer Tracy, and his favourite scriptwriter Alan Jay Lerner of *My Fair Lady* and *Gigi*. He had taken over making *Under the Clock* after another director had begun it and, trying to give this studio-bound film about New York a touch of realism, had provided each of the many extras with 'bits of character', thus instituting a practice which was to lead to his being described as 'extra-crazy'. The extraordinary scene in *Meet Me in St Louis*, where a camera sails up to a window and then, instead of halting there, apparently floats right through the glass pane, had been achieved by construction of a set in two sections which, at the critical moment, slid apart to admit the camera.

Minnelli himself, charming in an unworldly kind of way, seemed baffled that anyone could admire him as much as I clearly did. His wife, though, was thoroughly ready to be flattered on his behalf and, as I was about to leave, seized from a shelf a book that Minnelli had praised, with the somewhat morbid title of *A Funny Thing Happened on My Way to the Grave*, forced her dazed but compliant husband to autograph it and then, in her own hand, added the words: 'To the most charming English newspaper man!' – the nearest anyone has ever got to acknowledging me as a proper journalist. Interestingly, just as Kelly had been ungenerous about Donen, so Minnelli was ungenerous about Kelly and Donen. When I asked him who, apart from himself, he regarded as estimable directors of musicals, he pondered for a while and then replied that he could not think of anyone.

Having tasted Hollywood vicariously if fragmentarily, I was avid to experience the real thing. I had to wait for it but eventually, in 1976, the opportunity came. As a minister in the Labour Government in charge of the aircraft industry, I was asked to go to the United States to visit their three principal airframe manufacturers with an eye to possible collaboration. Two of these, Lockheed and McDonnell Douglas, had establishments in Los Angeles, and at last it seemed that I would be able to make the pilgrimage I had been working towards all my life.

Our plane landed at midnight. I was met by the British consul. He had worked out in meticulous detail a programme for my extremely short stay which, with lunches, press and radio interviews and speeches, left not a moment for the tiniest, briefest moment in Hollywood.

Definite measures would have to be taken, and taken right away. I therefore announced as we walked out of the air terminal that I wished to go to my hotel via Hollywood. 'Now, Minister?' queried the consul in astonishment. I glanced at my watch. It was almost exactly midnight. 'Yes, now,' I said firmly. One of the most estimable persons who has ever been a member of the public service now took a hand. On the flight from Seattle I had told the senior civil servant accompanying me, Ron Dearing, who later became chairman of the Post Office and was most properly knighted, that one of my dearest wishes was to see the junction of Sunset Boulevard with a street named Camden. In *Singin' in the Rain* Debbie Reynolds, as a dancer named Kathy Selden, had at a critical moment in the development of the plot given a lift in her car to Gene Kelly, playing Don Lockwood, a star of the silent screen. When she arrived at the destination he requested, Kathy sang out; 'Here we are! Sunset and Camden!' So when I had expressed my disconcerting wish to go to Hollywood without delay, Ron Dearing added in a Whitehall voice that brooked no refusal: 'And the Minister wishes to go via Sunset and Camden.'

It was clear to the consul and his driver that they were in the hands of maniacs, so without any further quibble off we went. The driver before long brought the car to an abrupt halt. 'This is Sunset and Camden,' he announced, though not as prepossessingly as Debbie Reynolds had done a quarter of a century before. The place, a steep, twisting road, looked nothing like the flat, straight street depicted on the MGM studio set, but all the same I felt a sense of acute satisfaction. Then, on we went to Hollywood Boulevard.

The consul warned me that the only reputable establishment open (there being numerous disreputable places which we could enter, mainly pornographic cinemas, none of which he could recommend) was a discount record shop, Tower Records, which never closed at any time on any day or night. Rather than simply peer at the neon signs on Hollywood Boulevard, I decided to have a brief look around the record shop. This proved to be enormous, and protected by rather threatening armed guards.

The shop's stock was not only massive but also tempting, and I picked up several desirable items, including a cassette of David Raksin conducting the scores he had composed for *The Bad and the Beautiful* and *Laura*, as well as extracts from soundtracks of Warner Brothers films of the 1930s. I then went to the counter to pay, offering my credit card to the sales clerk. 'Have you a California driver's licence?' he enquired. I was compelled to confess that I had not, a reply he had not anticipated, since it was almost certain that he had never in his life before met someone who did not possess a California driver's licence. He paused, and thought hard. 'Do you have any identification with your picture on?' he asked. I thumbed through my wallet, and came upon my House of Commons member's pass, from which stared my features at their most idealistic. I handed it over. He looked at it. He turned it over. He thought. 'What is this?' he asked. 'It's a pass to say that I am a member of the British Parliament.' He thought some more. He asked me to wait a moment. He went away.

He then returned in the company of a fat and clearly authoritative man. This senior official once again asked me to explain what my pass signified. Once again I said that it meant that I was a member of the British Parliament. He pondered. A light slowly flickered and then came on full. 'You mean like Harold Wilson?' he asked. 'Yes, like Harold Wilson,' I confirmed. The authoritative fat man turned to the sales clerk. 'Give the man the records,' he said.

'Either he's genuine, or else it's the best con I've ever known and he deserves to succeed.'

Triumphant, I went to the Los Angeles Hyatt Hotel for what was to be a short sleep – for the consul, with that clarity of comprehension which makes our foreign service what it is, now understood that it was essential for me to spend some time in Hollywood itself the next day, and had reorganized my programme in a way that, provided I got up early, would give me half an hour on Hollywood Boulevard by daylight. So next morning, between engagements, I was taken to Grauman's Chinese Theatre. There at last I saw for myself that famous oriental entrance. There at last I inspected on the pavement the hand- and footprints and signatures of cinema stars, some of them, like Clark Gable and Bette Davis, still celebrated, others, like the comedian Joe E. Brown, who also left his mouth print, almost completely forgotten. Sophia Loren provided an Italian inscription, Shirley Temple sent 'Love to you all'. It was a moment that could have been bathetic but turned out to be extremely touching. I wandered among those signatures as if through a necropolis, seeing in stone the different civilizations of the cinematic era stretching not over thousands of years but over no more than a couple of generations.

Then I was hauled off to visit an aircraft factory, and my only other taste of Hollywood was a momentary glimpse of the entrance to MGM studios as our car sped to the airport from which I was to return to England. Two years later I was back, this time on my own time and at my own expense, staying in Hollywood itself, in a Japanese motel in north Hollywood. On holiday in the American West, I had decided on a few days in Los Angeles. I went to Grauman's again. I wandered along the Boulevard, which was indeed as squalid as the consul had warned. I went into Larry Edmunds's Hollywood bookshop, the film bookshop above all other film bookshops, even more dingy than Cinemabilia and with assistants so surly as to make Cinemabilia's seem abjectly fawning. I bought a few things just for the sake of it.

I went to the Hollywood Bowl for a concert, just as I had seen people do in movies, and did my best to hear the Los Angeles Philharmonic play Mahler to the *obligato* accompaniment of bottles and cans being clanked by a huge audience in a vast amphitheatre. It was not a memorable concert but it was a cherishable experience.

Then I went to MGM. It had never occurred to me to go on the regulation studio tour at Universal, enjoyable as it was reported to be. Universal had no redolence for me. It was MGM I wanted to see and, since there were no arrangements for admission of the public, I had written to the company's president and asked if I could come and have a look round. He had replied with promptitude and in the affirmative and so, on the arranged day and at the arranged time, I at last arrived at Culver City and found West Washington Boulevard. There it was, the cream stucco group of buildings I had seen in so many photographs, with the funeral parlour next door. I walked into the Irving Thalberg Building, through the same entrance as Hepburn, Garbo, Norma Shearer, Eleanor Powell, Mickey Rooney, George Cukor, and Louis B. Mayer himself, had used. I was taken to the president's office past a corridor lined with the pictures of past stars and, after a few moments' conversation, was put in the hands of a woman from the publicity department.

We went downstairs and outside. The bar protecting the entrance to the studios itself was raised. We were in. MGM's backlot had, lamentably, been sold off long ago, but many sound-stages survived and I was taken into several of them, all looking exactly like the one in which Gene Kelly had sung 'You were meant for me' to the accompaniment of a wind machine and a studio spotlight. I was shown the sound-stage in which *An American in Paris* had been made. In all that huge studio, where once thousands of people had been at work, only one film was at the time being made, a musical with Luciano Pavarotti called *Yes, Giorgio* that turned out to be so bad that it was never properly released. Shuttled around the alleyways in a little electric cart, I saw the garishly lavish set for *Turandot* that had been constructed for that prospective fiasco, as well as an uncannily lifelike street scene that had been built for another failure, *Pennies from Heaven*. I was taken to the standing set for *Dallas*, MGM having been reduced to the humiliation of making space available for television series, and was shown how the scenery was built just a little smaller than life in order to make the performers look bigger.

My tour ended. The woman from the publicity department, who filled in the time with gossip from an era long before she had been at the studio (mostly gleaned, she told me, from the most knowledgeable person at MGM, the shoeshine man), clearly saw that it was a melancholy as well as a memorable occasion for me. I had come too late in the studio's history, but coming late was better than not coming at all. To round off my visit she took me to a little shop which sold small items to studio employees. Rummaging around, I decided to buy a blue T-shirt with, stamped on its front, the MGM lion surrounded by the dog-Latin motto 'Ars Gratia Artis' that the songwriter Howard Dietz had invented, and a red cap emblazoned with the same insignia. Clutching my trophies, I made my way back to West Washington Boulevard and back to reality.

CINÉMA VÉRITÉ

John L. Sullvian was a film director in the United States at the end of the 1930s. He was extremely successful at directing comedies with names like *Ants in the Pants*; but he came to feel that he ought to be more serious and socially conscious in his approach to picture-making, so he set out disguised as a hobo to see the world and gain a new perspective. He met with a series of misfortunes and eventually found himself imprisoned in a chain gang. Sitting one night in a makeshift cinema during a brief period of permitted leisure, he watched a Mickey Mouse cartoon. Looking around at his fellow-convicts and seeing them enjoying a rare moment of laughter, he realized that there was no greater boon that he as a film-director could bestow on his fellow-citizens than to make films that would provide a little escapism for them in their careworn lives.

From the time in the Rialto cinema, Leeds, when as a tiny child I saw the first frame of *The Three Little Pigs*, it did not occur to me that films were about anything but the pleasure of the moment. You went to see them, you sat through them, you emerged from the exit having pushed the appropriate bar on the green-painted metal door, and you forgot all about them. To see a film twice was so unheard-of as to be a sign of definite peculiarity. To regard a picture seen in the cinema as representative of an art form was absurd, art being the pictures on the walls of the City Art Gallery.

So I proceeded, with 'Blondie' films and 'William' films (disappointing those) until Richard Winnington came along to tell me that I had not been watching films the right way at all. Admittedly, movies might provide pleasure, but that was incidental to their doggedly serious objective of instructing (documentaries about erecting BBC masts were fine for that purpose) or, even more important, communicating a message about the nature of society and, if possible, an admonition about what should be done to put right the very many things which were undoubtedly wrong. This approach fitted snugly with my concurrent discovery of politics. I therefore made it my rule to go only to films which I could regard as 'serious'. To have a good time at the pictures was permissible provided that the pleasure was subsidiary to being uplifted or – more often, as it seemed – depressed.

I continued going to the cinema because it was almost impossible for me physically not to go to the cinema but, as that little ticket flipped out of its slot in the metal surface of the box-office counter, to be handed over to the usherette for tearing jaggedly in two, I was aware that I was engaged on serious business. It was for others, with less intellectual insight and less social responsibility than I possessed, to see pictures for the frivolous purpose of being entertained. I despised the reported remark of Samuel Goldwyn: 'If you want a message, try Western Union.'

I looked carefully, therefore, for films that had something to say. Russian films were especially good, because they had ever such a lot to say. French films were less overtly political, but they too seemed acceptable because they were so gloomy – literally so, in the case of movies directed by Marcel Carné which contained all those shadows and in addition were full of working men, mostly played by Jean Gabin wearing a cap. Italian neo-realist films qualified instantaneously, and so did the German post-war cinema, which included not only works suffused with remorse about the War but also cynical glances at the economic miracle, of which the most attractive was *Das Mädchen Rosemarie*. This latter mixed political comment with a story of a high-class prostitute, and told its story in a highly decadent way complete with songs which might have been written by Kurt Weill himself.

The Americans, it turned out, despite that evil studio system that I had been taught to despise, made quite a lot of political films too, of which John Ford's *The Grapes of Wrath*, about poverty in the depression, was the most famous or, to apply an adjective that seemed invented to describe something pretentious, 'distinguished'. Another of Ford's films, *The Last Hurrah*, which seemed to have a feel for the aroma of politics, was impregnated with the tang of electioneering.

Of course, I learned that electioneering in parts of the United States was very different from canvassing in Potternewton ward, Leeds. In Leeds we talked about demagogues; the Americans actually had them, particularly in the South, and made film after film about them. The one that gained the most recognition, and won several Oscars, was *All the King's Men*, with Broderick Crawford as the would-be dictator; but, while less well known, *A Lion Is in the Streets*, with James Cagney, seemed to me pretty well as good. There was another called *The Boss* starring John Payne and featuring a caricature of Harry Truman and yet another, *A Face in the Crowd*, directed by Elia Kazan and starring Andy Griffith.

American films dealing with politics seemed to go in cycles: now a series of witch-hunting films, with titles like *I Was a Communist for the FBI* and *I Married a Communist*, now a series of anti-witch hunting movies, such as *Three Brave Men*, with Ernest Borgnine as a Navy Department employee sacked for allegedly Communist views and *Storm Centre*, containing the indomitable Bette Davis as a librarian defending the integrity of her book-shelves. At least, however, American films were always aware – however cravenly or hypocritically or smugly or, occasionally, courageously – of the political world about them. Even comedies included political jokes. As zombies – the walking dead – advanced menacingly in *The Ghost Chasers* Bob Hope exclaimed, 'Look! Democrats!'

For years the British cinema appeared to be almost completely insulated from the political process. Occasionally there might come along a film that dealt safely with the politics of the past, like *Fame Is the Spur*, adapted from Howard Spring's novel about Ramsay MacDonald, or perhaps one that daringly featured a scene in the House of Commons, such as *The Years Between* with Valerie Hobson – herself to become the wife of a Conservative MP –as, of course, a Conservative MP who is the widow of a Conservative MP. When, in the 1950s, the British cinema did start dabbling in political controversy, it was generally from the right-wing point of view. *I'm All Right Jack*, hailed as a coruscating comedy, and *The Angry Silence*, respected as a profound tract, both represented trade unionists as ruffians who were at best fools and at worst knaves. Richard Attenborough, director of *The Angry Silence*, claimed the noblest motives for the film, but those motives were put on paper by a scriptwriter, Bryan Forbes, who later was to help with Conservative party political broadcasts. It has to be said, however, that if Forbes had combined the insight of Chekhov with the wit of Oscar Wilde, I would still have been doggedly prejudiced against him once I realized he was a Conservative supporter. I was committed – or bigoted – to the extent that I was ready to pillory the artistic efforts of a performer, a writer or a director, if his politics were not to my taste.

137

It was easy to form these judgments about Americans because in the United States those who made or appeared in films were often forthright about their party allegiances. Sometimes, though, I got them wrong. At first I thought that, because he made *The Grapes of Wrath*, John Ford was all right. As I saw some of his later films, I came to the conclusion that after all he was a reactionary, if not worse. How could it be otherwise when he was a close personal friend of John Wayne, and it was well known that Wayne was a fascist, or at the very least a semi-fascist? Even more repugnant was Adolph Menjou, member of right-wing activist groups; and nearly as bad, I was told, was Gary Cooper, whose casting in the film version of Ernest Hemingway's *For Whom the Bell Tolls* was regarded as an outrage against the pro-Republican intentions of that novel about the Spanish Civil War.

Spanish Republicans, then, were on the right side, namely my side. American Republicans, on the other hand, were totally to be deplored, and I was annoyed to find that Ethel Merman sang in support of their campaigns, distressed to discover that Ginger Rogers was an Eisenhower fan. Special scorn was reserved for Frank Sinatra who, having supported John Kennedy against Nixon, later switched sides and became a Nixon supporter.

Of course, the more I read about the odious activities of the Hollywood witch-hunt – one of the most lavishly documented episodes in all political history, with book after book providing new revelations or at any rate new gossip about old revelations – the more I despised those who had, in the jargon of the times, 'named names'. I was honest enough with myself to acknowledge that, if I had been in the predicament of having to decide whether to inform on my friends – if I had had to choose between my livelihood and my intregrity – I would have hoped to reject the role of an informer. However, I could not be absolutely sure how I would have behaved, faced with a real hard decision rather than a hypothetical, comfortable choice. All the same, this ambivalence did not prevent me harbouring the utmost scorn for those who had chosen the easy way, the craven way, and these unfortunates promptly entered my rogues' gallery. Larry Parks, whose *The Jolson Story* I would not have dreamt of seeing, became a hero because he was a victim; I found it even easier to sympathize with his wife, the gravel-voiced Betty Garrett, who had been such a delight as the taxi-driver in *On the Town* in 1949 and who, though she was rehabilitated in time to play the title part in the musical version of *My Sister Eileen* in 1955, had her bright film career brought to an end before she was 40 years old.

I never did like Burl Ives very much, so was not too put out (indeed, in a sense, felt vindicated for my mild antipathy towards him) when I learned that he had spilled the beans. The case of Edward Dmytryk was irritating because, after admiring his anti-anti-Semitic film *Crossfire*, I was so full of sympathy with him in his travails that, when he came to Britain as a political exile, I even went to see *Give Us This Day*, his awful melodrama full of symbolism about the Crucifixion. I therefore felt badly let-down when he decided to co-operate with the Congressional witch-hunters after all, and returned to the United States to resume his career with, I was prompt to decide, some pretty terrible pieces of work (among them *The Caine Mutiny* for which I conceived an irrational antipathy). I nurtured an especial detestation for Elia Kazan, one of the most willing informers of them all, especially when I understood that his *On the Waterfront*, which I had greatly admired, was intended as a justification for informing, cunningly scripted by a writer, Budd Schulberg, who had also co-operated with the villains of that period.

Political judgements about British stars were much more difficult to make, since performers on this side of the Atlantic did not, on the whole, flaunt their political allegiances. The revelation of Dora Bryan's Conservatism broke my heart, it is true. I hardened my heart against Vanessa Redgrave when she left the Labour party for the Workers' Revolutionary Party. Rosamund John's beauty seemed even greater when I learned that she actively campaigned for the Labour Party in, of all places, St. John's Wood.

There I was, then, absolutely sure of my opinions and ready to judge films and performers on the basis of their conformity to my prejudices. These were the days when I was scurrying about London, catching up on films of the past which I had missed, and one day I at last found a cinema that was showing an old movie by Preston Sturges, an approved director even though he specialized in comedies. The film was *Sullivan's Travels*, and told the story of John L. Sullivan, the director who was ashamed of making movies with titles like *Ants in the Pants*.

I was thrown into confusion, even turmoil. Here was a picture which I knew to be a classic, possibly the most considerable work of a director who, though he made comedies, made comedies with a social point to them. Here was a picture that certainly had a message, rammed home very hard. The problem was that the message undermined everything I had been taught about the acceptable motivations for film-making and film-viewing. What was more, I secretly agreed with the message that it propagated. I had not rejected the belief that films should be about something; but I was forcibly made to realize that the something that films might be about was, in addition to social criticism and political propaganda, the merits of simply having a good time.

Sullivan's Travels taught me a lot. It taught me, first, that humourlessness was an unforgivable sin. After all, had I not nodded approvingly in *Twelfth Night* when, playing Maria, I had heard my boy-friend Sir Toby Belch rebuke Malvolio: 'Dost thou think, because thou art virtuous, there shall be no more cakes and ale?' I was as sure as I ever had been that life was serious; but from then on I began to be even more sure that a serious life did not preclude joyousness, and that hedonism was a desirable aim of political action.

Sullivan's Travels taught me, too, that there was a place in art for everything; that being gloomy with Dreyer or Bresson was art, but that laughing uncontrollably at Groucho Marx or W. C. Fields was art too; that art did not have to be precious and self-conscious, but could be robust and outward-going; that the construction of a successful comedy routine took as much skill and subtlety as the final, heart-rendingly frustrating crowd scene of *Les Enfants du Paradis*. I learnt that it takes even more skill to make people laugh than to make them cry.

Most important of all, I came to realize that every film had a message, whatever that message was, whether a message was intended by the makers, or even if the makers did not actually know that they were concocting a message. Every work of art, however lowly, however unpretentious, however abysmal even, said something about the world, either through what it contained or through what it left out. I realized that students of a period could, indeed, learn more about the thoughts and assumptions of people living during that period from examination of its routine artistic artefacts than from its most consciously cerebral works. Archaeologists prize a crude potsherd as well as a cache of precious and elaborate jewels.

So, I saw, the daftest, even the most contemptible, films were telling their audiences something. Rubbish like the series of Anna

Neagle comedies – those named after select parts of London, such as *Spring in Park Lane*, *Maytime in Mayfair* and *The Courtneys of Curzon Street* – were brainwashing customers into accepting that the existing social order was fine and dandy, just as it should be, with the rich man in his castle and the poor man at the gate.

A lavish but boring musical like *Lady in the Dark*, Kurt Weill music and all, was telling women not to be rivals to men. The problem of the heroine – all those dream sequences of excruciating tedium she was forced to undergo – boiled down to her presumptuousness in assuming that she had the right to compete with men on equal terms. As one of the characters in the film protested: 'She shouldn't try to be top man. She's not built for it. She's flying in the face of nature.' Far better for Liza to give up her successful career and bend the knee to the man who knew what was best for her, even though the man was the simpering Ray Milland and the woman the mettlesome – despite her Republican sympathies – Ginger Rogers. Almost the identical theme, without the music, provided the plot for *June Bride*, with Bette Davis playing the Ginger Rogers role and Robert Montgomery, a Milland clone, complaining to her: 'Every time I get affectionate with you, I feel as though I were snuggling up to the Taft-Hartley Bill'. These pictures issued the same message that made *The Taming of the Shrew* the most difficult to stomach of all Shakespeare's plays and which the Nazis summed up in the slogan Kinder, Kirche, Küche.

Moreover, it was a woman's duty not only to stay at home, cook and have babies, but to look beautiful as well. Being beautiful was, indeed, the supreme achievement of any female, as was proved again and again by scenes in which a dowdy heroine took off her spectacles and revealed herself to be attractive after all. Where that left all the women who were not conventionally beautiful, that is, most women, was not explained.

Being good, even very good, at her job was for a woman no excuse. In fact the better she was, the worse it was, because she was outsmarting men at what only men were supposed to succed at. She demonstrated this error by wearing mannish clothes, especially tailored suits, and hats that looked like trilbies; in fact (like Bette Davis in *The Man Who Came to Dinner*, for example) she was dressed to resemble the popular conception of a lesbian – not that films during the 1940s and 1950s remotely hinted that there were such people as lesbians; indeed, Warners could make a movie called *I Was a Male War Bride* without the slightest hint from anyone that such a title might indicate sexual unorthodoxy.

A woman, in fact, was only expected to excel at her work if she was a fully-fledged genius – like Madame Curie, who could be forgiven for doing a man's job in a man's world because she discovered radium and, as a happy bonus, looked like Greer Garson into the bargain. In *Ziegfeld Follies* Judy Garland mocked this whole concept by playing Madame Crematon, the woman who invented the safety pin. The irony here was that Greer Garson herself had refused to perform in this satire, regarding such a proceeding as beneath her dignity. Judy Garland took over the role and demonstrated that she, so far from matching the accepted notion of charm that Louis B. Mayer called her 'my little hunchback', had fifty times the talent of the regal Miss Garson.

In the movies it was made plain that a woman's greatest ambition, conscious or subconscious, was to become a wife, as Liza managed to do by the end of *Lady in the Dark*. Once out of those androgynous tailored garments, she was revealed to be a smasher. Being a smasher, however, was, though advantageous, not indispensable. In *Marty* – actually lauded, when released in 1956, as a realistic social document – something even more incredible was proved, namely, that you could become a wife, and thus totally fulfil yourself, even if you were plain like Betsy Blair – although, having no great claims on any really attractive man, you might have to end up with a man who was ugly (Ernest Borgnine), who did such an unglamorous job as a butcher's, and who would woo with the flattering words, 'Dogs like us, we ain't such dogs as we think we are'.

Of course, there was a place in life for plain women who could not manage to get married, and that was to make wisecracks as companion to the pretty, marriageable female star. Eve Arden performed that function in cinema for nearly thirty years. The basic joke of *Tootsie*, made in the 1980s, was that an unhandsome man in disguise (Dustin Hoffman) could play this role. His desire when in male clothes to win the attractive heroine was represented as unrealistic because preposterous. The whole point of Woody Allen's comedies, even in this later liberated period, was to draw attention to the remarkable achievement of a mousy little man in winning pretty girls. Allen was the first comedian wearing spectacles even to contemplate such a possibility. No one ever imagined that Groucho Marx could obtain anyone better looking than

Margaret Dumont while she, with all the money she possessed in her screen roles, could hope for no one better than Groucho, who then satisfied the expectations film conventions had aroused by spurning her. Ronald Reagan might be regarded by a majority of American voters as fit to be President, but for Warner Brothers his lack of conventional good looks meant that as a film actor he could hope at most to be the hero's brother or best friend.

Marriage, said the cinema, was not only best but safest. Extra-marital affaires were doomed, and should therefore not even be entertained. Anyone who ignored this strict social rule was looking for trouble, trouble that might end up in murder, as demonstrated in movies adapted from stories by James M. Cain, *Double Indemnity* and *The Postman Always Rings Twice*. The former was directed by that allegedly most unconventional director-scriptwriter Billy Wilder, the latter exercised such an abiding fascination that it was filmed three times in thirty-five years and was still regarded as socially relevant in 1981. This most recent version was indeed the most graphic in depicting the squalor of surrendering to illicit sexual cravings. In both of these tales, and in numerous other variants, a hard, selfish woman's seduction of her fancy man into murdering her husband for gain was shown to be not only wrong but, even worse, unprofitable.

For, in cinema, not only was adultery depicted as taboo; crime certainly was not allowed to pay. Crime, indeed, was represented as a kind of sexual activity, a coitus interruptus where effort was not permitted to reach fulfilled climax. Film after film told the story of a robbery attempt which either failed in its execution (often as a result of the thieves falling out) or succeeded but was then frustrated. This moral lesson could be taught in drama form, as in *The Asphalt Jungle* or *The Killing*, or as a comedy, the much-lauded *The Lavender Hill Mob* being the same theme played for laughs. Indeed, not only crime but any kind of extravagant ambition was shown to be undesirable, as demonstrated in another Alec Guinness comedy, *The Man in the White Suit*, where the brainwave of the inventor, an impregnable clothing that never got dirty, attracted the bitter opposition of labour as well as capital.

Over and over again, the movies warned their viewers, 'Do not do anything unorthodox'. Picturegoers were told not to commit crime, and not to stray out of the herd in other ways. No good could come out of any unconventionality. Everyone should know his place in society and stick to it. In *Room at the Top* Laurence Harvey was shown to be a louse for wanting to escape from his restricted circumstances (a louse, moreover, who was shown to be doubly so for treating a loving woman badly in a foolish adulterous relationship). The higher he went, as the sequel *Life at the Top* proved, the bigger a louse he became. If you were not nasty, you knew your place. The most beloved films of Frank Capra, regarded as quite outspoken for their time, offered the message that the little man was acceptable as long as he remembered to stay little or, if he stopped being little for a specific and praiseworthy purpose, went back to being little once he had completed his task. Mr Deeds went to town, but Mr Deeds did not stay in town.

Cinema not only provided escapism for those living humdrum or deprived lives, but told those living humdrum or deprived lives that, really, they were much better off than the rich or adventurous, even when appearances might suggest the contrary. As time passed, and times apparently became less repressed, the message remained the same. *Bonnie and Clyde* ended up just as dead in 1967 as did the young lovers of *They Live by Night* in 1948, the admonitory story of this latter pair being regarded as sufficiently up-to-date to be told again under its original title, *Thieves Like Us*, in the supposedly liberated '80s.

This moral, 'Know your place', was indeed drummed into children from an early age. Possibly the most popular children's film ever made, *The Wizard of Oz*, ended with Dorothy proclaiming; 'There's no place like home.' Oz turned out to be made of tinsel, its magic a deception, its wizard a fraud. Kansas, however, was real, even though constricting, and everyone should stick to what they knew best. The most lucrative children's film ever made, *E.T.*, delivered precisely the same message more than forty years later, with the hideous but adorable homunculus croaking the word 'home' until every child in the neighbourhood entered into a conspiracy to get him there. For even adventurous young people knew what was what. *Breaking Away*, a film about rebellious youth in the late 1970s, featured as its hero a teenager so unorthodox as to pretend to his baffled Middle Western parents that he was really Italian. It ended with the members of the rebel group soberly acknowledging their responsibilities as members of society.

Even when no clear message was apparent or even intended, cinema was about a society of consensus. Always, movies indicated, more often than not subliminally, that authority was to be respected. Authority, indeed, was so awesome that often it could not even be depicted as human. A shadow, a silhouette, the back of a head were all that audiences were generally permitted to see of Stalin in Russian films, of Roosevelt in American movies, of King George in British wartime pictures; although earlier English sovereigns were fair game, Queen Elizabeth being remote enough in time to qualify as a fictional character, while Queen Victoria, after Anna Neagle did her the honours, was transmuted into material for a meaty, often comic, character role.

Moreover, when the movie makers did demonstrate how courageous they were being, they tended to do so in the safest way. In the anti-anti-semitic film *Gentleman's Agreement*, the Jew was really a Gentile, so that was all right. In *Crossfire*, where a real Jew was the murder victim, even that concession concealed cowardice, since the book on which the film was based featured the murder not of a Jew but of a member of an even more unpopular minority, a homosexual. *Pinky* was not about the plight of a black girl in a white world, but about the problems of a girl who was black biologically but looked white, and indeed was played by the white actress Jeanne Crain. In the various versions of *Showboat* the role of Julie, a woman with mixed blood, was played by white actresses. Lena Horne, whose film career was effectively brought to an end when she was denied this role, had foolishly ignored her father's warning, when he reluctantly financed her fortune-seeking trip to Hollywood, that black women could only hope to play maids.

The most unorthodox writer-directors stayed carefully within the system. As late as *Kiss Me Stupid*, Billy Wilder was still warning against adultery even though, by 1964, he was allowed to depict it. Preston Sturges himself was regarded as a rebel against the system. In *Hail the Conquering Hero* he satirized popular notions of heroism, and in *The Miracle of Morgan's Creek* he appeared to excuse, if not precisely vindicate, motherhood out of wedlock. Both of these films were comedy all the way. *Sullivan's Travels*, however, was more serious than Sturges's usual products. Its message, too, turned out to be conventional. Life, it said, is too serious to be wasted on serious matters. People, it advised, with great seriousness, do not want to be serious. *Sullivan's Travels*, indeed, was an argument against rebellion, in favour of predominant social values. It, too, just as much as *The Wizard of*

Oz, told its audiences that home was best, even when home consisted of a movie studio where unprovocative comedy films were made. The film that said that films did not need to have messages, indeed were better for not having messages, was itself a message film.

After seeing it, I went with an easy conscience to films apparently purveying pure entertainment. I was persuaded that movies did not always have to be solemn, and as a result saw far more films than I would have done otherwise. This was all to the good, because it is impossible to understand why the good is good until one sees lots of the bad, difficult to penetrate to the heart of one extraordinary film until one has seen dozens of ordinary films which have no heart. *Sullivan's Travels* brainwashed me; but later, without in any way revising my opinion as to its estimable qualities, I came to owe it a particular debt. Instead of stopping me thinking, it made me think more until, indeed, I saw through it.

II

FADE-OUT

———

'I *am* big. It's the *pictures* that got small.'

Norma Desmond, faded star of the silent screen, played by Gloria Swanson in *Sunset Boulevard*, reacted with haughty indignation when faced with the accurate implication that her stature in the cinema had diminished since the heyday of her popularity. In fact in 1950, when *Sunset Boulevard* was made, the movies were – depending on which way you looked at them – as big or as small as they had been a generation earlier. By the 1980s they had, in one sense, got much bigger.

True, there were far fewer of them. Those few, however, cost much more to make than the most expensive films of earlier years, some of them, indeed, consuming almost unimaginable fortunes belonging to, or borrowed by, their producers. An intimate musical, made entirely in the studio, *One from the Heart*, bank-rupted its progenitor, Francis Ford Coppola, because of the intricate technical devices employed and because, too, audiences very wisely refused to sit in front of it and be sent frantic by its tedium. Some exceptionally expensive films made profits more appropriate to astronomy than to cinematography; others ruined their directors' bankability – the ability to attract investors' money – though occasionally, like *Heaven's Gate*, became at any rate cult classics.

Almost all movies of the 1980s cost huge sums, and most of them showed it. When *Gone with the Wind* came to Leeds, we regarded it with awe because we knew that it lasted no less than three hours and forty minutes, and actually had an interval in the middle. In those days the running-time of most pictures was eighty, ninety or a hundred minutes and, as a result, the films were tautly and economically edited; they had to be, because audiences expected a second feature as well as all the other ingredients, ranging from organ to cartoon, of a long evening out. Forty years later, the slightest of comedies was expected to last well over two hours, because programme construction demanded such a length. In went the audience, bustled rather than ushered, and, following some commercials and perhaps a perfunctory trailer, they were plunged into the main film. Some pictures lasted for hour upon hour, and the word 'intermission', categorized in the Shorter Oxford Dictionary as 'rare', became a misused but regularly employed part of the English language.

Yet, longer though they were, more expensive though they were, the movies did in fact look smaller. This was partly because, with the exception of a handful of cinemas in the West End of London and even fewer auditoria elsewhere, most picture houses in Britain consisted of small halls, sometimes containing only a few dozen seats. Vast picture palaces had been split up into multiple exhibition centres, consisting of nooks and crannies of the original cinemas cut off from the other parts of the building by gimcrack partitions. People would sit in what used to be the circle, watching a different film from that shown in what used to be the stalls, while in a former foyer yet a third movie would be exhibited. Because the auditoria were smaller, the screens were far smaller too. When audiences entered Odeon One or Studio Three, instead of being overpowered by a vast wall of moving faces, as in former days, they were faced with an image so minuscule that it diminished even the biggest scene.

On the other hand, despite the massive expense, not many scenes in these films were all that complex. Projection in a cinema was now only part of a movie's life-cycle. Often just a few months after its première in a picture house, a major production would be available on cassette from video shops or libraries and, not too long afterwards, would be shown on the publicly available television channels having already, quite likely, been exhibited on pay-channels in hotels and elsewhere. So movie images had to be composed to be comprehensible on a tiny screen.

Millions grew up with an attitude towards watching films entirely different from that which had been inculcated into audiences of the 1930s, 1940s and 1950s. Far more saw films at home, on television or video-tapes, than in cinemas. The image on the screen, far from being almost hypnotically dominant as the only thing to be seen in an auditorium otherwise almost impenetrably darkened, became just one thing to look at in a room full of other things to look at. The image was, moreover, quite small in relation to those other objects even on the biggest television screens generally available. Instead of watching the activities of giants, viewers glanced without overmuch attention at the antics of pygmies. Instead of concentrating on the only available image, a television viewer glanced around the room, thought of other things, conversed with others watching with him, got up and made tea or had a snack, his gaze alternating from plate to screen and back again. The image was one item among many, dwarfed by the attitude of the watcher, instead of being all that could be seen, dwarfing the viewer. There was an impression, sometimes powerful, but no impact.

Not only was the nature of new films, tailored for ultimate showing on television, changed by these new conditions. The effect of televising old films, made in the days when movies were only projected on to big screens in large cinemas, was to diminish them. Some were butchered. Films made for CinemaScope had their ends sheared off, those made for other wide-screen systems such as VistaVision had their tops and bottoms sliced off; the marvellous dances choreographed especially for CinemaScope in *It's Always Fair Weather*, for example, suffered amputation and lost their meaning when shown on television. Older films whose proportions were appropriate to the shape of the television screen fared little better. Dance or crowd scenes intended to be shown as gigantic images lost all impact when substantially reduced in size. Parents who promised their children a treat when a television showing of one of their old favourites was announced were bewildered or hurt when the film turned out not to be as they remembered it, with their children either indifferent or contemptuous. Yet these children were the mass audience, the ones who watched television many hours a day for every day of the year, who when they went abroad sat in hotel lounges watching foreign television even though the language might be incomprehensible; any television image was enough for them. Meanwhile, the cinema audience shrank. It was for this reason that the huge picture palaces were broken up into units sometimes not much bigger than the normal living-room in a private home. Yet even in these mini-auditoria attendances might be so sparse that a handful of ticket-holders huddled together like refugees which, in a sense, is what they were.

Just as the reaction to films at home was different from that in the cinema, so the reaction to films shown in small cinemas was different from the reaction to those shown in the remaining picture palaces. I saw the original version of *Close Encounters of the Third Kind*, for me the best of Steven Spielberg's films and the most beautiful of all movies about incursions from other planets, as one of a packed audience in the circle of the Odeon, Leicester Square, where it was projected on to a huge screen. At the end, the sense of awe and happiness was such that people just sat where they were, unwilling to break the spell by moving. I saw the Special Edition of the same film, issued some time later, as one of a handful of people in one of the exiguous auditoria of the Odeon, Swiss Cottage. Not only did it leave such people as were present, including myself, completely cold; the experience spoiled for me the memory of my earlier viewing.

The impact of film comedy, in particular, altered. Funny films, to be effective, need a lot of people laughing together. Laughter interacts, enjoyment is enhanced, when the occupants of a crowded auditorium all regard the same joke or situation as very amusing. Individual viewers lack the self-confidence to laugh when no one else is laughing with them; they feel foolish when theirs is the only chuckle they hear.

The changing nature of the cinema altered the behaviour of the audience too. The end of the mass movie public spoiled what had once been the memorable experience of going to the movies. As a boy in Leeds I used to set out to the cinema in excitement. The main question, as I sat on the tram that was taking me into town, was: will there be a queue? Queuing was part of the entertainment, even though it involved great tension. There we stood, hundreds of us neatly in line, waiting for people to come out (in the middle of the film, of course) so that in small groups we could trickle in. Then came the end of the big picture, crowds streamed out of the front entrance, more from the exits at the side, none of them giving anything away by their facial expressions about the quality of what they had just seen.

After an agonizing wait the commissionaire, always a burly man of middle age, generally with a bristling moustache and dressed in a dauntingly authoritative uniform sometimes adorned with mysterious medals, would admit the queuers batch by batch. The nervousness grew. Would he put his hand up, to indicate that no more would be let in? Would he call out 'Singles only at one-and-nine', thus precipitating a debate in our group as to whether we should split up to re-unite later in the cinema itself. Would he announce 'One-and-nines full. Three-and-six only'? In that latter disastrous case, we would suspect that in fact there

were many seats left in the one-and-nines and that the commissionaire was attempting to fill the three-and-sixes. However,
there was no way to find out except by paying three-and-six, a
sum of money we did not have. So, with many others, we would
disperse in disappointment.

By the 1980s there was no problem about getting in, or finding
a good seat once in. Sometimes there was a queue, but this was
generally caused by confusion about which of four auditoria a
particular box-office dealt with, sometimes by the lack of comprehension on the part of the beautiful Oriental girl taking the
money. If all tickets at one price were sold out, everyone seemed
able to afford the higher prices. Indeed, curiously, the most
expensive seats were often sold out first.

In the forlorn partitioned buildings that used to be temples of
pleasure, the ambience became quite different from what it used
to be. Many cinemas, suburban as well as those in city centres,
became purveyors of refreshments on a substantial scale. All
manner of evil-smelling 'fast foods' were available, together with
cardboard containers of soft drinks and crackling packets of
popcorn. Even the most august establishments, for example the
once-sumptuous Empire, Leicester Square where the cream of
MGM's products had been shown, were sometimes turned into
squalid slums as customers tried to kick their way through the
detritus of the container society. Struggling through to the auditorium, they found themselves surrounded by groups of young
people behaving like a modified version of a football crowd.
Those young people were, for the most part, not deliberately
unruly. They did not resemble the occasional groups I used to
encounter in Leeds, where good-natured rowdyism had to be
quelled by a man with a stick. They were the norm, not the
exception, and it did not occur to cinema managements that they
needed to be silenced in the interest of the enjoyment of the rest
of the audience.

When I was a child, going to the cinema was an occasion; by
the time I was middle-aged, it was regarded simply as a variant of
watching television for which it was necessary to leave home; but
the informality of home viewing, including casual conversation
and the consumption of food and drink, had been transferred to
public viewing. Once, when in my teens, I was rebuked in Leeds
Town Hall, where I was attending a concert by the Yorkshire
Symphony Orchestra, for behaving in too animated a way (talking

during the overture, I think) and thus violating 'concert manners'. The audiences of the 1980s had not been brought up to have cinema manners, because they were not part of the cinema generation. The same cinema audiences included those of the new video generation who watched films in the same more casual and less reverential way and were no more put out by their neighbours' rowdiness than their neighbours were by theirs.

For the mass screen audience had gone. Instead, the cinema-going audience, vastly reduced in numbers compared with thirty or forty years ago, was divided into separate groups which rarely came together. Those who went to see the works of Wim Wenders or Satyajit Ray were unlikely to be found watching something as genteel as *On Golden Pond*, let alone *Conan the Barbarian*. Again and again people over forty could be heard almost boasting, 'I can't remember the last time I went to the pictures'.

When people did go to the cinema, they went in distinct and separate batches. While the great stars of the halcyon days still survived, there was a dwindling minority who would struggle through the popcorn packets to see what, say, Katharine Hepburn or Bette Davis was doing. Foreign language films had their *afficionados*, even fewer than in previous generations. For the rest, film audiences were composed of adolescents going on their own and relatively small children being taken for treats.

All the big stars, the last survivors of the days of stardom as it once was, were ageing, with no newcomers to take their places. In the era of the Hollywood studio system, stars were groomed and, indeed, created like factory products. True, some attempts at manufacturing stars, like Samuel Goldwyn's gallant attempt to deify Anna Sten, capsized. Many, however, were spectacular successes. Clark Gable, Robert Taylor, Greta Garbo, Lana Turner, all became international names because of the careful grooming they received from MGM, but it is highly unlikely that the modest acting talents of any of them except Garbo would have been noticed without the publicity and influence of a giant studio. Spencer Tracy might have had a solid career in Broadway plays. Judy Garland's enormous talent – Gene Kelly told me that in his view she was 'the finest performer we've ever had in America' – would almost certainly have forced its way through to public acclaim as Barbra Streisand's did a generation later; but, just as Streisand hardly made a film of real quality, so it is likely that Garland's brilliance would have been encased in mediocrity.

In the 1970s and 1980s there were faddish stars, who lasted a little while, but who were unknown to people who did not visit the cinema, that is, the majority of the population. There were no stars who could sell fan magazines, so there were no mass-selling fan magazines. It was impossible to imagine Richard Gere, Dustin Hoffman, Dolly Parton or Bo Derek causing riots by their presence, in the way that Chaplin, Robert Taylor or, as late as the 1950s, Marilyn Monroe did. The major superstars of the 1980s – Robert Redford, Paul Newman – were venerable relics of the studio system; there were no young superstars who lasted for more than a handful of years. John Travolta began as a sensation and, almost immediately, became a has-been. Once he graduated from teen-fodder like *Saturday Night Fever* and *Grease* to a film of quality, Brian de Palma's *Blow-Out*, his fans ditched him and moved on to someone else. There was no one to shape his career except himself, and he did not know how. Louis B. Mayer would have given him a long-term future. The last great representative of youth, Elvis Presley, died in 1977, fat and ugly, aged 42; in the 1980s he was adulated more than anyone who came after him. The greatest superstar of them all, Elizabeth Taylor, ceased making films entirely and turned her private life into a star role instead.

The most lucrative films – indeed, the most profitable films made in the history of the cinema – were produced with children, often small children, in mind. Children liked to see these films several times and, more often than not, adults had to take them, their presence thus increasing receipts. These pictures were frequently extraordinarily expensive to make, often put together with spectacular technical ingenuity. However, Joseph Mankiewicz was cruelly accurate in describing them as cartoons. For that is what they were, cartoons with people, mostly inexpensive people who were paid small salaries, leaving most of the budget available for the bewitching special effects which had superseded Disney animation.

Few of their almost innumerable audiences could have named the stars of *Star Wars* or *E.T.*, or even *Flash Gordon* (who, in fact, was played by a former *Playgirl* centrefold). *E.T.* might well still be played in the twenty-first century, but its re-appearance would not arouse nostalgic love for its child protagonists in the way that each revival of *The Wizard of Oz* renewed affection for Judy Garland. *Raiders of the Lost Ark*, followed by *Indiana Jones and the Temple of Doom*, did publicize the name of the actor who played Indiana Jones, but few conceived that he had an existence, let alone a future, outside that one role in the way that Sean Connery could supply performances of real merit when cast other than as James Bond.

Nor did these cartoon films need directors of individualistic talent so much as capable supervisors and editors. True, Richard Lester, a quirky individual, tried to add sparkle to the *Superman* sequel that he directed, just as Steven Spielberg of *E.T.* was capable, if required, of providing style in *Close Encounters of the Third Kind* and, though not required or indeed desired, of taking risks with his one major failure, *1941*, a heavy-handed but genuinely inventive fantasy based on the imagined Japanese invasion of Los Angeles.

Spielberg, like his friend George Lucas, responsible for the 'Star Wars' series, was in fact an *auteur* who destroyed the *auteur* theory. Able to exercise supreme power over their films, such directors did so not by permeating them with individuality but by draining them of it. Just as the days of the stars and the days of the studios had been of limited duration, so were the days of the *auteurs*. A coterie of admirers might go devotedly to see films by the Germans Rainer Werner Fassbinder and Werner Herzog, but few directors any more had the large public that would go to see pictures made by Hitchcock or de Mille.

Of the innovators of the French New Wave, Jean-Luc Godard got lost in the byways of far-left ideology and must have been frustrated to see the success that established him, *Breathless*, remade a quarter of a century later as a semi-pornographic American thriller. Louis Malle, whose *Les Amants* was regarded as almost intolerably erotic in its time (1958), entered the international mainstream with a dazzling thriller, *Atlantic City*, in 1982 and followed it with a comparable – if less successful – effort, *Crackers*, in 1984. Only Francois Truffaut, whose *Les Quatre Cent Coups* was to me the undisputed masterpiece of the New Wave and whose *Fahrenheit 451* was the loveliest and the most genial futurist film until *Close Encounters of the Third Kind* (in which he himself appropriately appeared) continued to make small films in his own way. He died appallingly young, after directing a series of charming but somehow half-baked films like *Day for Night* and *The Last Metro* which everyone treated kindly and which got by on their irresistible good nature, if sometimes on little else.

In the United States the only *auteur* who went distraughtly on

154

his way devising relatively small-scale products for sophisticated urban audiences was Woody Allen. Although his film about a man with a chameleon personality, *Zelig*, consisted of a series of technical tricks, Allen's public on the whole went to see his films not because he directed them but because he also performed in them. In this preference they showed discernment because it turned out that his most successful work, *Annie Hall*, for which he won an Academy Award, was never intended by him to be about Annie Hall, nor to be called *Annie Hall*, but after completion in a very different form was reshaped for him by a discerning editor. It was, in a sense, satisfying that a work which apparently vindicated the *auteur* theory should have in fact exploded the *auteur* theory, but it gave credence to the view that the most commercially successful films of the 1970s and the 1980s were made by committees, even if, like all such bodies, these committees had a chairman.

Annie Hall won a Hollywood award but, though it was an American film, and although for half a century American films had mostly been Hollywood films, this was not a Hollywood film. Just as the British film industry was dead, occasionally showing signs of life after death with much-lauded safe stodge like *Chariots of Fire* and *Gandhi*, and replays of old Ealing comedies such as *Local Hero* (a slipshod and ill-constructed successor to Ealing's *The Maggie*, with its blundering American intruder shown how to live life at a sensible pace by eccentric but wise Scots), so Hollywood had become almost as much a ghost town as those I visited on my way back from Lamy.

It was a ghost town because its echoing sound stages were often completely empty of activity, and if used at all were being rented (as I saw at MGM) by parasitic television companies. Universal Studios operated highly successful tours, but these were patronized by people who did not often go to the movies any more and who went for a taste of the cinema as it used to be even though their experience of that cinema was limited to late-night television viewing. Hollywood was a ghost town in another way, too. It lived off its dead and with its dead. Larry Edmunds's shop on Hollywood Boulevard, like other film bookshops, had a steady trade in old posters and stills, rather like a cathedral souvenir stall selling reproductions of holy relics.

Of the few films made, a high proportion were parasitic – or cannibalistic – in their derivation from films of the golden age of cinema. Some were remakes, often of pictures, like *The Big Sleep*, *The Lady Vanishes* and *The Thirty-Nine Steps*, that it was effrontery if not sacrilege to try to emulate, sometimes of movies that should not have been made even once. The *Late Show*, a completely new and entertaining thriller, was a pastiche of old B movie thrillers. New films unashamedly quoted from old ones as, for example, *Raging Bull* battened off *On the Waterfront*. *Star Wars*, though its juvenile audience would never know it, was a collection of parodies of earlier film genres, and included a classic Western saloon brawl conducted by inter-galactic monsters. In his pictures Truffaut deliberately paid homage to Hitchcock. In *The American Friend* Wim Wenders allusively included the Hollywood cult directors Nicholas Ray and Samuel Fuller in his cast. In the remake of the cult film *Invasion of the Body Snatchers*, a minor role was played by Don Siegel, director of the original version. In *Against All Odds* (1984) a middle-aged Jane Greer played the mother of the girl she herself had portrayed in 1947 in *Out of the Past*, of which *Against All Odds* was an inferior remake. The Indiana Jones films were based on defunct serials for children. *Movie Movie*, the most inventive film for years, directed by Stanley Donen, was a wry but loving pastiche of two genres of films made in the thirties, the musical and the gangster picture, both opening with precisely the same stock shot of a New York street sign. The cinema in its decline was feeding off its past, feeding off itself.

A vast nostalgia industry grew up, a nostalgia extraordinary in its yearning for such a very short period. Postcards of yesterday's stars, today's legends, were eagerly bought by people who had not been born when those stars were at their zenith. The British Film Institute announced as its calendar for 1985 twelve stills from the films of the fifties, each still 'accompanied by a caption giving details of the film and setting it in the context of the period'. Films of the 1950s had become period relics by the mid-1980s. Record shops in every continent had their movie nostalgia sections. There were even some shops that sold nothing but nostalgia records, and seemed to make a profit. I bought out-takes from MGM musicals in Manchester and, in Lucerne, a collection of rare recordings of Marilyn Monroe which put that lady in her true historical perspective: 'Happy Birthday and Thanks for the Memory. From the 1962 birthday party for President Kennedy in Madison Square Garden. President Kennedy also heard.'

I do not go to the pictures very often these days. Am I losing interest? No; it is just that I want to go on seeing the kind of films I have always enjoyed, and few of these are being made any more. Not all that many films of any kind are being made, and of those new movies that are shown there are not many that, when I read the reviews, I really feel I want to see. I try, I really do. From time to time I will make the effort and go to some work by a director whose work I am assured is worth watching. I went, for example, to see Wim Wenders's screen adaptation of *The American Friend*, lured by the information that it was based on one of the 'Ripley' books by Patricia Highsmith. I sat through it conscientiously, not really enjoying it, which I am sure was all right since it did not seem to have been made to be enjoyed, and it certainly did not have all that much to do with the book I had read. I recalled with some poignancy that I had only ever started reading Highsmith's 'Ripley' books because of the marvellous René Clement thriller *Plein Soleil*, based on the first of this amoral adventurer's exploits, and that I had only heard of Patricia Highsmith in the first place because Alfred Hitchcock based *Strangers on a Train* on another of her novels.

I went to – and enjoyed – *Blow-Out* because I thought that I ought to go and see at any rate one film directed by Brian De Palma, and all the others I had read about sounded too bloody (literally) for me. I could not, though, bring myself to see *The Deer Hunter* because I did not want to flinch at the Russian roulette scene. I believe strongly in the making of serious films, but I do not want to see films that gratuitously depict violence and suffering, which is why I avoided some highly-praised movie showing a man getting his nipple pierced. I am, I admit it, squeamish. I have no particular objection to pornography being available in films for those who want pornography. I saw Derek Jarman's homosexual film with Latin dialogue, *Sebastiane*, and at any rate was able to check that my Latin had not got rusty. Conscientiously, I then went to see his adaptation of Shakespeare's *The Tempest*, found it contained a modicum of nudity, but thought it inadequate to the point of vacuity as a version of Shakespeare. That was enough Jarman for me.

In Nice on a package tour with an elder sister, I searched the newspaper for something worth seeing at the pictures and could find nothing except what appeared to be a hard-porn movie. We agreed to go, but agreed also that we would leave as soon as one of us had had enough. From the moment the picture began, several people of both sexes, all nude, began doing forward and familiar things to each other, employing numerous parts of their bodies in the process. After a few minutes they seemed to have run out of things to do, and simply started doing them all over again. A new experience became humdrum within minutes. Turning to my sister to signal our exit, I found that she had turned at the same time to me. We went out into the darkness and completed the evening with ices topped with Chantilly cream.

The shade of Richard Winnington hovering over me with finger raised in admonition, I carefully considered a visit to Taviani's *Padre Padrone*, but the promised scene of bestiality deterred me. I would have seen the dissident films from Turkey if I could have been promised that there would be no scenes of torture, the fear of which kept me away from *Midnight Express* which in any case I was assured was simply a commercial exploitation movie. I felt that if I was to continue regarding myself as a conscientious movie-goer, I ought to see at any rate one film made by John Boorman, was attracted by the sound of *Excalibur*, and found myself watching a farrago that would have been farcical had it not been so tedious. Yet it was highly praised, as too was *Local Hero*: the standards of criticism have fallen to match the levels of cinematic achievement.

I go. I hope; but rarely do I get the thrill – of excitement, of terror, of amusement, of visual adventure – that I used to experience so often. I am ready to seize and relish it when it comes. I was dazzled by the opening sequence of Akira Kurosawa's *Kagemusha*, possibly the most exciting opening sequence in all cinema, with a breathless warrior running down, down, down an interminably long flight of steps. Having become somewhat irritated with Andrzej Wajda's fictional films, out of solidarity with Solidarity I went to see his semi-documentaries about the struggle for democratic rights in Poland, *Man of Marble* and *Man of Iron*, and found myself much moved.

Occasional wonderful surprises like these encourage me to continue seeing new films, and will keep me going to the cinema for as long as I can fight my way through the popcorn packets and endure the conversations of my neighbours. An addiction remains an addiction, and whenever I go I still dare to tell myself that this time it will be special. However, in my heart I know that the game is up. I know that I am certain to get more pleasure from

watching a second-rate Claudette Colbert revival at the National
Film Theatre than anything that Mel Brooks is conceivably
capable of making, that one sequence with Franklin Pangborn is
funnier than every film that Dudley Moore has ever starred in,
that Monty Python is not fit to wipe *Hellzapoppin*'s boots, that
Woody Allen being so determinedly serious in *Interiors* tells me
less about life than Vittoria de Sica being comic in *Miracle in
Milan*.

It is even doubtful whether the cinema has a future at all. The
video revolution has only just begun. Recorded visual entertainment will increasingly be experienced in the home, and the
environment will dictate the content. Films made for public
exhibition before mass audiences will no doubt continue to be
made for a while, though in dwindling quantities, with a widening
gap between the pretentious films for sophisticates and the live-
action cartoons for children. One day, however, they are likely to
peter out. The last Odeons will close, perhaps turned into video
libraries rather than bingo halls. A tiny number of specialist
cinemas, whose total is already gravely depleted, may struggle on
for a while. Large populated centres may retain one cinema
auditorium as a public service, in the same way that they feel it
proper to provide museums and art galleries, so that this transitory
form of entertainment may be available for sampling by those
who would otherwise be unable to know what it was like.

However, those unfortunates will never really know what it was
like. They will never know the thrill of going into that foyer with
its strange aroma, of stumbling into their seat in the dark, of
seeing the curtains part, of watching the blackness of the screen
illuminated by that lion, that shield, that mountain, that searchlight, of getting ready to see something new, something mysterious,
something wonderful. That thrill has almost disappeared. When
it finally vanishes, it will never return. People will not lack for
entertainment, for theatres performing great plays new and old,
opera houses, concert halls, and the visual arts of the future. They
will, though, have lost something precious that helped shape
millions of lives as it certainly shaped mine, making it richer,
better-informed and, above all, happier.

The sound film, the talkie, as a mass entertainment that
dominated the world, lasted more or less for a third of a century, a
tiny sliver in the history of mankind. It is my priceless good
fortune that I was there at the time.